YORK NOTES

A CHRISTMAS CAROL

CHARLES DICKENS

WORKBOOK BY BETH KEMP

YORK PRESS
322 Old Brompton Road, London SW5 9JH

PEARSON EDUCATION LIMITED
Edinburgh Gate, Harlow,
Essex CM20 2JE, United Kingdom
Associated companies, branches and representatives throughout the world

First published 2016

10 9 8 7 6 5 4 3

ISBN 978–1–2921–3807–7

Illustrations by Kay Dixey; and Alan Batley (page 48 only)

Phototypeset by DTP Media
Printed in Slovakia

Photo credits: © iStock/D Leonis for page 11 / © iStock/Pesky Monkey for page 13 / woe/Shutterstock for page 19 / © iStock/duncan1890 for page 23 / © iStock/wbritten for page 25 / revers/Shutterstock for page 29 / © Northscape/Alamy Stock Photo for page 33 / Everett Historical/Shutterstock for page 35 / © The National Trust Photolibrary/Alamy Stock Photo for page 46 / krcil/Shutterstock for page 53 / Kao-len/Shutterstock for page 61

CONTENTS

PART FOUR:
THEMES, CONTEXTS AND SETTINGS

PART FIVE:
FORM, STRUCTURE AND LANGUAGE

PART SIX:
PROGRESS BOOSTER

PART ONE: GETTING STARTED

Preparing for assessment

HOW WILL I BE ASSESSED ON MY WORK ON *A CHRISTMAS CAROL*?

All exam boards are different but whichever course you are following, your work will be examined through these three Assessment Objectives:

Assessment Objectives	Wording	Worth thinking about ...
AO1	Read, understand and respond to texts. Students should be able to: • maintain a critical style and develop an informed personal response • use textual references, including quotations, to support and illustrate interpretations.	• How well do I know what happens, what people say, do, etc? • What do I think about the key ideas in the novella? • How can I support my viewpoint in a really convincing way? • What are the best quotations to use and when should I use them?
AO2	Analyse the language, form and structure used by a writer to create meanings and effects, using relevant subject terminology where appropriate.	• What specific things does the writer 'do'? What choices has Dickens made? (Why this particular word, phrase or paragraph here? Why does this event happen at this point?) • What effects do these choices create? Suspense? Ironic laughter? Reflective mood?
AO3	Show understanding of the relationships between texts and the contexts in which they were written.	• What can I learn about society from the novella? (What does it tell me about poverty and inequality in Dickens's day, for example?) • What was society like in Dickens's time? Can I see it reflected in the text?

Look out for the Assessment Objective labels throughout your York Notes Workbook – these will help to focus your study and revision!

The text used in this Workbook is the New Windmills edition, 1992.

How to use your York Notes Workbook

There are lots of ways your Workbook can support your study and revision of *A Christmas Carol*. There is no 'right' way – choose the one that suits your learning style best.

1) Alongside the York Notes Study Guide and the text	2) As a 'stand-alone' revision programme	3) As a form of mock-exam
Do you have the York Notes Study Guide for *A Christmas Carol*? The contents of your Workbook are designed to match the sections in the Study Guide, so with the novella to hand you could: ● read the relevant section(s) of the Study Guide and any part of the novella referred to; ● complete the tasks in the same section in your Workbook.	Think you know *A Christmas Carol* well? Why not work through the Workbook systematically, either as you finish sections, or as you study or revise certain aspects in class or at home. You could make a revision diary and allocate particular sections of the Workbook to a day or week.	Prefer to do all your revision in one go? You could put aside a day or two and work through the Workbook, page by page. Once you have finished, check all your answers in one go! This will be quite a challenge, but it may be the approach you prefer.

HOW WILL THE WORKBOOK HELP YOU TEST AND CHECK YOUR KNOWLEDGE AND SKILLS?

Parts Two to **Five** offer a range of tasks and activities:

These fun and quick-to-complete tasks check your basic knowledge of the text.

These more open questions challenge you to show your understanding.

This task focuses in on a key character, theme, tecÚique, idea or relationship and helps you plan and write up paragraphs for an essay.

A clear, quick way to visually record your progress

Each Part ends with a **Practice task** to extend your revision:

An exam-style task for you to practise a full essay

Practice task

① First, **read** this **exam-style** task:

Read the first three paragraphs of the novella, from: 'Marley was dead: to begin with.' to 'solemnised it with an undoubted bargain.' (p. 1)

Question: Which aspects of the novella does Dickens set up in this opening passage?

② Begin by circling the **key words** in the **question** above.

③ Now complete the table, noting down **3–4 key points** with **evidence** and the **effect** created:

Point	Evidence/quotation	Effect or explanation

④ **Draft your response**. Use the space below for your first paragraph(s) and then continue onto a sheet of paper:

Start: *In this extract, Dickens introduces various aspects of the novella which will become important. Firstly, …*

PROGRESS LOG [tick the correct box]   Needs more work ☐   Getting there ☐   Under control ☐

36 A Christmas Carol

A plain table provided for you to fill in with your own ideas

The first sentence of the essay provided for you to use as a prompt to start a full-length essay

Part Six: Progress Booster helps you test your own key writing skills:

A sample of a student's writing challenges you to judge its strengths and weaknesses.

Structure and linking of paragraphs   (A01)

Paragraphs need to demonstrate your points clearly by:

- Using **topic sentences**
- Focusing on **key words** from quotations
- Explaining their **effect** or meaning

① Read this model paragraph in which a student explains how Dickens presents the Ghosts:

Dickens presents the Ghosts as guides who help Scrooge learn from the scenes he is shown. They sometimes highlight his previous bad behaviour in order to do this, for example, repeating Scrooge's words back to him and calling him an 'insect'. This teaches Scrooge how insignificant he is and demonstrates to him that he does not have the right to judge or criticise others.

Look at the response carefully:

- **Underline** the topic sentence which explains the main point about the Ghosts.
- **Circle** the word that the Ghosts use to describe Scrooge.
- **Highlight** the part of the last sentence which explains the word.

② Now read this paragraph by a student who is explaining how Dickens presents Fred:

We learn more about Fred when he is talking to his family about Scrooge: 'He may rail at Christmas till he dies, but he can't help thinking better of it – I defy him – if he finds me going there, in good temper, year after year, and saying Uncle Scrooge, how are you?' This tells us what kind of person Fred is.

Expert viewpoint: This paragraph is unclear. It does not begin with a topic sentence to explain how Dickens presents Fred and does not zoom in on any key words that tell us what Fred is like.

Now **rewrite the paragraph**. Start with a **topic sentence**, and pick out a **key word or phrase** to 'zoom in' on, then follow up with an **explanation** or **interpretation**:

Dickens presents Fred as

62 A Christmas Carol

It is equally important to make your **sentences link together** and your **ideas follow on** fluently from each other. You can do this by:

- Using a mixture of short and long sentences as appropriate
- Using words or phrases that help connect or develop ideas

③ Read this model paragraph by one student writing about Scrooge and how he is presented:

Dickens presents Scrooge as an older man who seems very set in his ways. At the start of the novella, his ideas about Christmas and other people appear very fixed, for example when he refuses to help 'idle people', suggesting that he has no sympathy for the poor whatsoever. By the end of the novella, he is transformed. The insights the Ghosts give him into other people's lives make it impossible for him to continue to dehumanise them, which changes his outlook completely.

Look at the response carefully:

- Underline the topic sentence which introduces the main idea.
- Underline the short sentence which signals a change in ideas.
- Circle any words or phrases that link ideas such as 'who', 'when', 'implying', 'which', etc.

④ Read this paragraph by another student also commenting on how Scrooge is presented:

Dickens creates a clear image of some aspects of Scrooge's appearance. This is found in Stave One. He is described as 'his eyes red, his thin lips blue' and 'A frosty rime was on his head, and on his eyebrows, and on his wiry chin.' All this is because he has his own 'cold within him'. This suggests what an uncaring and callous man he is. He always makes everywhere cold because he is such an unfeeling person.

Expert viewpoint: The candidate has understood how the character's nature is revealed in his appearance. However, the paragraph is rather awkwardly written. It needs improving by linking the sentences with suitable phrases and joining words such as: 'where', 'in', 'as well as', 'who', 'suggesting', 'implying'.

Rewrite the paragraph, improving the **style**, and also try to add a **concluding sentence** summing up Scrooge's character and appearance.

Start with the same **topic sentence**, but extend it:

Dickens creates a clear image of some aspects of Scrooge's appearance …

PROGRESS LOG [tick the correct box]   Needs more w

An expert teacher or marker's view of the student's work will help you understand key skills.

An opportunity for you to apply what you have learned to a new point

Don't forget – these are just some examples of the Workbook contents. Inside there is much, much more to help you revise. For example:

- lots of samples of students' own work at different levels
- help with writing skills
- advice and tasks on writing about context
- a full answer key so you can check your answers
- a full-length practice exam task with guidance on what to focus on.

PART TWO: PLOT AND ACTION

The Preface & Stave One, pages 1–3: Dickens, Scrooge and Marley

QUICK TEST ✓

1 Which of these are **TRUE** statements about this section, and which are **FALSE**?
Write 'T' or 'F' in the boxes:

a) The Preface shows that Dickens wrote this story simply to entertain. `F`

b) There are hints that this will be a ghost story. `T`

c) The first point in the story is that Marley, Scrooge's partner, is dead. `T`

d) Scrooge narrates the story. `F`

e) We learn that Scrooge is a cold person emotionally. `T`

f) Scrooge is working on Christmas Eve. `T`

THINKING MORE DEEPLY ?

2 Write **one** or **two sentences** in response to each of these questions:

a) What do you think is the purpose of the Preface?

....

....

....

....

....

b) Why do you think Dickens writes so much about Marley?

....

....

....

....

c) What do we learn about the weather in this part of Stave One?

....

....

....

....

....

EXAM PREPARATION: WRITING ABOUT SCROOGE

A01

Read from *'Scrooge knew he was dead?'* (p. 1) to *'better than an evil eye, dark master!'* (p. 3)

Question: How does Dickens introduce the character of Scrooge here?

Think about:

- How Scrooge is described
- How others respond to Scrooge

3 Complete this table:

Point/detail	Evidence	Effect or explanation
1: *Dickens shows us that Scrooge was not particularly upset by Marley's death, despite their close relationship.*	*'Scrooge was … his sole friend and sole mourner. And even Scrooge was not so dreadfully cut up'*	*The repetition of 'sole' emphasises the isolation of Scrooge and Marley; Dickens makes Scrooge's reaction to Marley's death more shocking by placing it in a new sentence.*
2: *Dickens explains how other people avoid Scrooge.*		
3: *Dickens uses detailed description and imagery to present Scrooge's character.*		

4 Write up **point 1** into a **paragraph** below in your own words. Remember to include what you infer from the evidence, or the writer's effects:

....

....

....

....

....

5 Now, choose **one** of your **other points** and write it out as another **paragraph** here:

....

....

....

....

....

PROGRESS LOG [tick the correct box]   Needs more work ☐   Getting there ☐   Under control ☐

Stave One, pages 3–10: Scrooge has visitors

QUICK TEST ✔

❶ Complete this **gap-fill paragraph** about this section, with the **correct or suitable information**:

Scrooge does not seem to .... his clerk, Bob Cratchit, as he does

not allow him to have the coal near him. Scrooge's ...., Fred, visits

him to wish him '..................... ....', but Scrooge replies with

'.....................!' and '.....................!' Scrooge thinks that Fred is foolish to

celebrate and says 'what reason have you to be merry? You're ....

enough'. Fred replies that Scrooge should therefore be happy as he is

.... Fred thinks of Christmas as a .... time but cannot

convince Scrooge. After he leaves, two .... gentlemen visit to try to

collect money for the Poor. Scrooge shocks them by suggesting that if the Poor

would rather .... than go to prison or the workhouse, they should do it

and .... the .... population.

THINKING MORE DEEPLY

❷ Write **one** or **two sentences** in response to each of these questions:

a) What do we learn about Scrooge and Bob Cratchit from their journeys home?

....
....
....
....

b) What do you think is the purpose of the carol singer in this scene?

....
....
....
....

c) Why does Dickens make Scrooge talk about workhouses and the Poor Laws?

....
....
....
....

EXAM PREPARATION: WRITING ABOUT ATMOSPHERE

A02

Read from *'Meanwhile the fog and darkness thickened'* (p. 8) to *'the baby sallied out to buy the beef.'* (p. 9)

Question: How does Dickens use language to set the scene in this section?

Think about:

- What happens and how it is described
- How it relates to the main plot

3 Complete this table:

Point/detail	Evidence	Effect or explanation
1: *The weather worsens, becoming foggier, darker and colder.*	*'overflowings sullenly congealed, and turned to misanthropic ice'*	*This choice of vocabulary reminds the reader of Scrooge, who is both 'sullen' and 'misanthropic', associating him with cold and with being separated from others.*
2: *Dickens presents a series of festive snapshots, reminding the reader that it is Christmas Eve.*		
3: *Dickens creates an image of everyone else getting ready to celebrate, in contrast with Scrooge.*		

4 Write up **point 1** into a **paragraph** below in your own words. Remember to include what you infer from the evidence, or the writer's effects:

....

....

....

....

....

5 Now, choose **one** of your **other points** and write it out as another **paragraph** here:

....

....

....

....

....

PROGRESS LOG [tick the correct box]   Needs more work ☐   Getting there ☐   Under control ☐

Stave One, pages 10–20: Marley's Ghost

QUICK TEST ✔

1 **Circle** the correct answer to **complete the quotation**:

a) 'there was nothing at all [particular / special / unusual] about the knocker on the door' **(p. 10)**

b) 'Marley's face ... had a dismal light about it, like a bad [cheese / beef joint/ lobster] in a dark cellar' **(p. 11)**

c) 'A slight disorder of the [mind / stomach / digestion] makes them [i.e. the senses] cheats' **(p. 15)**

d) 'I wear the chain I [forged / made / created] in life' **(p. 16)**

e) 'The common welfare was my business: charity, mercy, forbearance, and [beneficence / benevolence / benediction], were, all, my business.' **(p. 18)**

THINKING MORE DEEPLY ?

2 Write **one** or **two sentences** in response to each of these questions:

a) Why do you think Dickens insists so many times and in so many ways that Scrooge is not a character who is prone to flights of fancy?

....

....

....

....

....

b) Why do you think Dickens refers to Marley as 'the Ghost'?

....

....

....

....

c) What is the key purpose of this Stave?

....

....

....

....

....

EXAM PREPARATION: WRITING ABOUT JUSTICE   A02

Read from *'Scrooge fell upon his knees'* to *'It is a ponderous chain!'* (p. 16)

Question: How does Dickens create tension around the idea of justice?

Think about:

- Scrooge's reaction to Marley
- Marley's message for Scrooge

❸ Complete this table:

Point/detail	Evidence	Effect or explanation
1: *We see that Scrooge is frightened and uncertain.*	*'Scrooge fell upon his knees'*	*Dickens shows how Scrooge's reactions to Marley's revelations grow stronger and stronger as he becomes more disturbed.*
2: *The construction of Marley's chains is described.*		
3: *The idea of punishment or justice is introduced.*		

❹ Write up **point 1** into a **paragraph** below in your own words. Remember to include what you infer from the evidence, or the writer's effects:

....
....
....
....
....
....

❺ Now, choose **one** of your **other points** and write it out as another **paragraph** here:

....
....
....
....
....
....
....
....

PROGRESS LOG [tick the correct box]   Needs more work ☐   Getting there ☐   Under control ☐

Stave Two, pages 21–5: The Ghost of Christmas Past

QUICK TEST ✔

1 Which of these are **TRUE** statements about this section, and which are **FALSE**? Write '**T**' or '**F**' in the boxes:

a) Scrooge wakes to find that it is dark, and when the clock strikes 12, he does not understand, since it cannot be noon. ☐

b) Dickens does not continue describing the weather in this section. ☐

c) Scrooge is unconcerned about Marley's Ghost at this point. ☐

d) The first thing Scrooge sees of the Ghost of Christmas Past is a hand drawing back the bed curtains. ☐

e) The Ghost wears a white tunic and holds a bunch of holly. ☐

f) The Ghost's belt shines out a constant bright light. ☐

THINKING MORE DEEPLY ?

2 Write **one** or **two sentences** in response to each of these questions:

a) Why do you think Dickens tells us that Scrooge stayed up until after 2 a.m. and yet the clock is striking midnight?

....

....

....

....

....

b) Why do you think Dickens puts himself into the story with 'as close to it as I am now to you'?

....

....

....

....

....

c) Why does Scrooge want the Ghost to put its cap on?

....

....

....

....

....

EXAM PREPARATION: WRITING ABOUT THE GHOST OF CHRISTMAS PAST A02

Read from *'It was a strange figure'* (p. 23) to *'at a distance.'* (p. 24)

Question: How does Dickens create a sense of this Ghost being related to the past?

Think about:

● How the Ghost is described

● The effect on the reader

3 Complete this table:

Point/detail	Evidence	Effect or explanation
1: *The Ghost's physical appearance recalls all ages at once.*	'like a child: yet not so like a child as like an old man'	*This phrasing encourages the reader to see the Ghost as representing an entire lifespan all at once: the whole past of an individual.*
2: *Dickens refers to distance more than once in describing the Ghost.*		
3: *Dickens emphasises the Ghost's qualities of indistinctness and impermanence.*		

4 Write up **point 1** into a **paragraph** below in your own words. Remember to include what you infer from the evidence, or the writer's effects:

....

....

....

....

....

5 Now, choose **one** of your **other points** and write it out as another **paragraph** here:

....

....

....

....

....

....

PROGRESS LOG [tick the correct box]   Needs more work ☐   Getting there ☐   Under control ☐

Stave Two, pages 25–30: Scrooge's unhappy childhood

QUICK TEST ✔

➊ Complete this **gap-fill paragraph** about the section, with the **correct or suitable information**:

The Ghost takes Scrooge into the .... and the atmosphere shifts:

the .... clears and Scrooge's mood changes too. The Ghost asks

Scrooge why his voice is .... and there are several hints that he is

.... Scrooge and the Ghost visit a schoolroom, passing several happy

and excited .... on the way. Inside the school, just one boy remains,

engrossed in ...., as characters from the stories appear at the window.

The scene shifts to a year later: the same boy, Scrooge, is again .... in

the school, when his sister, Fan, bursts in to tell him that his .... has

decided that he can return home for Christmas and that he is to become a man.

THINKING MORE DEEPLY ❓

➋ Write **one** or **two sentences** in response to each of these questions:

a) Why does Dickens make the weather in this scene different from the story so far?

b) How does Dickens begin to create more sympathy for Scrooge at this point?

c) What does it mean that Scrooge is 'to be a man'?

EXAM PREPARATION: WRITING ABOUT SCROOGE'S FAMILY **A01**

Read from *'It opened'* (p. 28) to *'and answered briefly, "Yes."'* (p. 30)

Question: How does Dickens present Scrooge's family in this section?

Think about:

- The language used to describe Fan's behaviour and appearance
- Scrooge's response to the mention of Fred

3 Complete this table:

Point/detail	Evidence	Effect or explanation
1: *Dickens presents Fan as small and lively.*	*'clapping her tiny hands, and bending down to laugh'*	*Dickens's descriptions of Fan centre on verbs such as 'darting', 'bending' and 'laughing', showing how she is constantly active.*
2: *Fan is described as a loving sister, keen to have Scrooge back home.*		
3: *Dickens portrays Scrooge as troubled when the Ghost mentions his nephew.*		

4 Write up **point 1** into a **paragraph** below in your own words. Remember to include what you infer from the evidence, or the writer's effects:

....

....

....

....

....

5 Now, choose **one** of your **other points** and write it out as another **paragraph** here:

....

....

....

....

....

....

....

PROGRESS LOG [tick the correct box]   Needs more work ☐   Getting there ☐   Under control ☐

Stave Two, pages 30–4: Fezziwig's party

QUICK TEST ✔

1 **Circle** the correct answer to **complete the statement**:

a) Scrooge immediately reacts in an [excited / upset / emotional] way to seeing Fezziwig again.

b) Dickens shows us how [unhappily / willingly / carefully] Young Scrooge works for Fezziwig when he and Dick Wilkins put up the shutters.

c) Fezziwig's staff clear the office floor in order to have a party for [staff / family / lots of different people].

d) Fezziwig and his wife are [clumsy but enthusiastic / skilled and energetic / not very keen] dancers.

e) Scrooge witnesses himself as a young man and the other apprentice discussing Fezziwig, and he begins to feel [guilty / angry / sad] about how he has treated Bob Cratchit.

THINKING MORE DEEPLY ?

2 Write **one** or **two sentences** in response to each of these questions:

a) How does Dickens's presentation of Fezziwig's physical appearance support his character?

....

....

....

....

b) Why do you think Dickens takes the time to list the work that went into preparing the room?

....

....

....

....

c) How do you think readers are intended to respond to Scrooge's little speech about Fezziwig's 'power to render us happy or unhappy' on page 34?

....

....

....

....

EXAM PREPARATION: WRITING ABOUT GENEROSITY   A03

Read from *'In came a fiddler'* (p. 31) to *'had no notion of walking.'* (p. 33)

Question: How does Dickens use Fezziwig's party to promote the ideas of benevolence and generosity?

Think about:

● What happens in this scene and how it is described

● How the text relates to Dickens's society

3 Complete this table:

Point/detail	Evidence	Effect or explanation
1: *We see that Fezziwig has invited many who could be seen as deserving or disadvantaged.*	*'the boy from over the way, who was suspected of not having enough board from his master'*	*Dickens models virtuous behaviour through Fezziwig – it is much more effective than preaching to the reader.*
2: *Dickens uses repetitive structures in his writing in this passage.*		
3: *Dickens seems to want to focus on the relationship between apprentices and their masters or mistresses in this part of the story.*		

4 Write up **point 1** into a **paragraph** below in your own words. Remember to include what you infer from the evidence, or the writer's effects:

....

....

....

....

....

5 Now, choose **one** of your **other points** and write it out as another **paragraph** here:

....

....

....

....

....

....

PROGRESS LOG [tick the correct box]   Needs more work ☐   Getting there ☐   Under control ☐

Stave Two, pages 34–9: The broken engagement

QUICK TEST ✔

1 Which of these are **TRUE** statements about this section, and which are **FALSE**? Write 'T' or 'F' in the boxes:

a) Young Scrooge's fiancée, Belle, breaks off their engagement because she has found someone else. ☐

b) Young Scrooge disappoints his fiancée by loving money more than he loves her. ☐

c) Belle explains to Young Scrooge that if they had met each other now, she would not have fallen in love with him. ☐

d) The Ghost also shows Young Scrooge a scene from the more recent past where Belle is married with children. ☐

e) Dickens as narrator appears again as this point to tell us about how happy Belle's family seems. ☐

THINKING MORE DEEPLY ?

2 Write **one** or **two sentences** in response to each of these questions:

a) Why do you think Dickens shows us Belle breaking off the engagement?

....
....
....
....

b) Why do you think the narrator's voice appears again here?

....
....
....
....
....

c) Why do you think Scrooge presses the extinguisher-cap down on the Ghost's head at the end of this scene?

....
....
....
....

EXAM PREPARATION: WRITING ABOUT SCROOGE

A01

Read from '"Belle," said the husband,' (p. 38) to the end of the Stave (p. 39).

Question: How does Dickens construct a sense of Scrooge's changing character in this section?

Think about:

- How others see Scrooge
- How Scrooge speaks and behaves

③ Complete this table:

Point/detail	Evidence	Effect or explanation
1: *Belle's husband is struck by Scrooge's isolation.*	*'Quite alone in the world'*	*Dickens shows that Belle's husband does not think of Scrooge as anything to do with himself or his family: he is merely an object of gossip, having isolated himself by his attitudes.*
2: *Scrooge wants to get away from the scene; he has had enough of the Ghost's visions.*		
3: *Scrooge appears to act without thinking in his panic at this point.*		

④ Write up **point 1** into a **paragraph** below in your own words. Remember to include what you infer from the evidence, or the writer's effects:

....

....

....

....

....

⑤ Now, choose **one** of your **other points** and write it out as another **paragraph** here:

....

....

....

....

....

....

....

PROGRESS LOG [tick the correct box]   Needs more work ☐   Getting there ☐   Under control ☐

Stave Three, pages 40–7: The Ghost of Christmas Present

QUICK TEST ✓

1 Complete this **gap-fill paragraph** about the section, with the **correct or suitable information**:

Scrooge awakens just before the clock strikes .... and pulls back the curtains around the bed in readiness for the next Spirit. The narrator assures us that he is ready for ...., but he is not ready for....................., which is what appears. Eventually, Scrooge gets up to investigate a .... which is streaming onto the .... from the next room, to find a mass of greenery, a piled-up feast and a 'jolly ....'. He is taken around the streets to see people making final preparations for Christmas. Some are taking their dinners to the .... to be cooked, as they do not have an oven. The Spirit has a torch, from which he sprinkles incense onto some people and their ....

THINKING MORE DEEPLY ?

2 Write **one** or **two sentences** in response to each of these questions:

a) Why do you think Scrooge appears unafraid of the Ghost at the start of this Stave?

....

....

....

....

b) How does Dickens use colour in this section?

....

....

....

....

c) Why do you think the Spirit applies incense to the poor people the most?

....

....

....

....

....

EXAM PREPARATION: WRITING ABOUT CONTEXT **A03** ✐

Read from '"*Spirit,*" *said Scrooge*' (p. 46) to '*not us.*' (p. 47)

Question: How does Dickens explore the impact of social policies on the poor in this extract?

Think about:

- What Scrooge says and how the Spirit reacts
- How these ideas are presented

3 Complete this table:

Point/detail	Evidence	Effect or explanation
1: *Scrooge argues against closing eating establishments on Sundays because the poor may not be able to eat well on other days.*	'often the only day on which they can be said to dine at all'	*This encourages the reader to think about why poorer families would find it difficult to 'dine' on the other days of the week.*
2: *The Spirit is offended that Scrooge blames him for this.*		
3: *Dickens makes the Spirit list a number of sins which are committed by humans and blamed on the Spirits.*		

4 Write up **point 1** into a **paragraph** below in your own words. Remember to include what you infer from the evidence, or the writer's effects:

....
....
....
....
....

5 Now, choose **one** of your **other points** and write it out as another **paragraph** here:

....
....
....
....
....
....

PROGRESS LOG [tick the correct box]   Needs more work ☐   Getting there ☐   Under control ☐

Stave Three, pages 47–53: Christmas at the Cratchits

QUICK TEST ✓

1 **Circle** the correct answer to **complete the quotation**:

a) Mrs Cratchit is '[dressed up / brave / pretty] in ribbons' (p. 47)

b) two smaller Cratchits 'came [tearing / racing / screaming] in' (p. 47)

c) Tiny Tim 'gets [worried / gloomy / thoughtful] sitting by himself so much' (p. 49)

d) The goose is '[eked out / supported / complemented] by the apple sauce and mashed potatoes' (p. 50)

e) The pudding is 'like a speckled [football / cannon-ball / orange]' (p. 50)

f) Scrooge is named 'the [Founder / Father / Foreman] of the Feast' (p. 52)

THINKING MORE DEEPLY ?

2 Write **one** or **two sentences** in response to each of these questions:

a) What impression do we get of the Cratchits' family life?

b) Why is it significant that Mrs Cratchit resists toasting Scrooge?

c) Why does the Spirit use Scrooge's words here about the 'surplus population'?

EXAM PREPARATION: WRITING ABOUT SOCIAL CLASS

A01

Read from *'After it had passed away'* to *'until the last.'* (p. 53)

Question: How does Dickens present the Cratchits' social position in this passage?

Think about:

- The content of the passage
- How the Cratchits are described

3 Complete this table:

Point/detail	Evidence	Effect or explanation
1: *The Cratchits are amused by the idea of Peter working in business.*	*'The two young Cratchits laughed tremendously at the idea of Peter's being a man of business'*	*Dickens shows us that even though the family needs the money, it is not the most important thing to them and they are a happy family even without it, unlike Scrooge.*
2: *The world of work and business is presented as separate and unfamiliar to the Cratchits.*		
3: *Dickens contrasts their poor appearance with their cheerfulness and obvious love for one another.*		

4 Write up **point 1** into a **paragraph** below in your own words. Remember to include what you infer from the evidence, or the writer's effects:

....

....

....

....

5 Now, choose **one** of your **other points** and write it out as another **paragraph** here:

....

....

....

....

....

....

PROGRESS LOG [tick the correct box]   Needs more work ☐   Getting there ☐   Under control ☐

Stave Three, pages 54–64: Christmas everywhere; Ignorance and Want

QUICK TEST ✓

1 Which of these are **TRUE** statements about this section, and which are **FALSE**? Write 'T' or 'F' in the boxes:

a) The Spirit shows Scrooge that miners who work deep underground do not celebrate Christmas. ☐

b) Scrooge sees men minding a lighthouse celebrating Christmas. ☐

c) Scrooge is taken to his nephew Fred's house, where Fred is mocking Scrooge, sneering cruelly at his inability to enjoy Christmas. ☐

d) Fred and his family conclude that Scrooge ultimately punishes himself with his attitude. ☐

e) Scrooge gets more and more irritated watching Fred and his family playing games. ☐

f) At the end of the Stave, Scrooge notices two ragged children hiding under the Spirit's robe: Ignorance and Want. The Spirit says they belong to Man. ☐

THINKING MORE DEEPLY ?

2 Write **one** or **two sentences** in response to each of these questions:

a) Why do you think Dickens describes so many different people celebrating Christmas in this Stave?

....
....
....
....

b) How do you respond to Fred's views about Scrooge here?

....
....
....
....

c) Why do you think Dickens repeats Scrooge's words back to him here?

....
....
....
....
....

EXAM PREPARATION: WRITING ABOUT IGNORANCE AND WANT   A02

Read from *'Forgive me if I am not justified'* (p. 63) to the end of the Stave (p. 64).

Question: How does Dickens present the roles of Ignorance and Want

Think about:

- How the characters of Ignorance and Want are described
- How Scrooge reacts to them

3 Complete this table:

Point/detail	Evidence	Effect or explanation
1: *Dickens presents Ignorance and Want as appalling and frightening creatures, emphasising how they are different from what children should be.*	*'Where angels might have sat enthroned, devils lurked'*	*Dickens presents these characters as corrupted or twisted by what has happened to them. They could have been happy, healthy children, but Man has made them terrifying creatures.*
2: *Scrooge is shocked at their appearance and does not know what to say.*		
3: *Dickens created these characters to argue that humanity has created the problem of poverty (want) through a lack of education (ignorance).*		

4 Write up **point 1** into a **paragraph** below in your own words. Remember to include what you infer from the evidence, or the writer's effects:

....

....

....

....

....

5 Now, choose **one** of your **other points** and write it out as another **paragraph** here:

....

....

....

....

....

PROGRESS LOG [tick the correct box]   Needs more work ☐   Getting there ☐   Under control ☐

Stave Four, pages 65–75: A man has died

QUICK TEST ✔

1 **Number** the events in this section so that they are in the **correct sequence**. Use **1** for the first event and **6** for the final event:

a) Scrooge states that he is more frightened of the Ghost of Christmas Yet to Come, and that he is resolved to change. ☐

b) Scrooge asks to see anyone who feels 'emotion caused by this man's death' and is shown a family who owed him money and are now relieved that they will have longer to pay. ☐

c) The Spirit takes Scrooge to a very poor and rough part of town, where they see three people trading items stolen from the dead man. ☐

d) Scrooge and the Spirit see businessmen discussing the death of a colleague. ☐

e) The Phantom arrives. It does not speak to Scrooge. ☐

f) The thieves express criticism of how the dead man lived, although they feel that he has made it easier for them to steal from him. ☐

THINKING MORE DEEPLY ?

2 Write **one** or **two sentences** in response to each of these questions:

a) In what ways is the Ghost of Christmas Yet to Come different from the previous ones?

....

....

....

....

b) What evidence is there at this point that the dead man could be Scrooge himself?

....

....

....

....

c) Why do you think Dickens includes the scene with the young couple in debt?

....

....

....

....

EXAM PREPARATION: WRITING ABOUT MONEY

A02

Read from *'Why then, don't stand staring'* (p. 70) to *'Ha, ha, ha!'* (p. 73)

Question: How does Dickens use language to convey a moral message in this scene?

Think about:

● How the thieves talk about the dead man

● How the dead man's possessions are described

③ Complete this table:

Point/detail	Evidence	Effect or explanation
1: *The thieves suggest that the dead man should have formed more relationships in life, in order to have people to leave things to.*	*'If he wanted to keep 'em after he was dead … why wasn't he natural in his lifetime?'*	*Even the thieves see the dead man's behaviour as unnatural, which they believe makes him fair game for their thievery.*
2: *Dickens uses vocabulary describing value and cost in presenting what the thieves' haul is worth.*		
3: *Dickens suggests that the dead man's behaviour has ultimately benefited only the thieves, as no one cares enough to notice their theft.*		

④ Write up **point 1** into a **paragraph** below in your own words. Remember to include what you infer from the evidence, or the writer's effects:

....

....

....

....

....

⑤ Now, choose **one** of your **other points** and write it out as another **paragraph** here:

....

....

....

....

....

....

....

PROGRESS LOG [tick the correct box]   Needs more work ☐   Getting there ☐   Under control ☐

Stave Four, pages 76–80: Tiny Tim and Scrooge's gravestone

QUICK TEST ✔

1 **Circle** the correct answer to **complete** the **statement**:

a) Scrooge and the Spirit find Mrs Cratchit making excuses about the [light / colour / smoke] straining her eyes.

b) Bob seems to be walking home more slowly than usual despite [not carrying Tiny Tim / being late / being sad].

c) The Cratchits all make an effort to be [helpful / gentle / cheerful] with one another.

d) Bob describes the place where Tiny Tim is to be [buried / treated / remembered] as a very green place.

e) Bob relates how he was touched by Fred's [memory / kindness / speech].

f) Scrooge is shown the grave of the man whose death he learned about earlier in the Stave: it is [green / clean / neglected] and is overgrown.

THINKING MORE DEEPLY ?

2 Write **one** or **two sentences** in response to each of these questions:

a) How does Dickens prepare the reader for the absence of Tiny Tim?

....

....

....

....

....

b) Why do you think Dickens includes a mention of Fred in this scene?

....

....

....

....

....

c) Why is Scrooge surprised that his future does not look very happy?

....

....

....

....

....

EXAM PREPARATION: WRITING ABOUT TINY TIM   A02

Read from *'But however and whenever we part'* to *'thy childish essence was from God!'* (p. 78)

Question: What is the role of Tiny Tim in the novella?

Think about:

- How he is spoken about here
- What is associated with him

3 Complete this table:

Point/detail	Evidence	Effect or explanation
1: *Tiny Tim's influence on the lives of others is long-lasting and has a profound effect.*	*'we shall none of us forget poor Tiny Tim'*	*Tiny Tim is discussed in affectionate terms, with the family using absolute and definitive language such as 'shall' and 'none of us'. Dickens clearly intends Tiny Tim to live on in readers' memories.*
2: *Bob Cratchit remembers Tiny Tim's good qualities.*		
3: *Tiny Tim's role is to remind everyone to be grateful and happy, no matter what their situation is.*		

4 Write up **point 1** into a **paragraph** below in your own words. Remember to include what you infer from the evidence, or the writer's effects:

....

....

....

....

....

5 Now, choose **one** of your **other points** and write it out as another **paragraph** here:

....

....

....

....

....

....

PROGRESS LOG [tick the correct box]   Needs more work ☐   Getting there ☐   Under control ☐

Stave Five, pages 81–5: A new beginning for Scrooge

QUICK TEST

1 Which of these are **TRUE** statements about this section, and which are **FALSE**? Write '**T**' or '**F**' in the boxes:

a) Scrooge is relieved to find his bed-curtains in place as this proves that, as far as he is concerned, he can still be saved. ☐

b) Scrooge does not believe what he has experienced and has to go around the house pointing out where the various Ghosts appeared. ☐

c) Scrooge is surprised at first to find that it is Christmas Day – and then delighted to find he can still make things right for this year. ☐

d) Scrooge calls out to a boy on the street to arrange to buy a huge goose for Bob Cratchit's family. ☐

e) Scrooge enjoys strangers wishing him a 'Merry Christmas'. ☐

f) Scrooge bumps into the charity collector who visited his office the day before and makes a large donation. ☐

THINKING MORE DEEPLY

2 Write **one** or **two sentences** in response to each of these questions:

a) What is the meaning of Scrooge's statement, 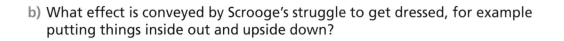'I will live in the Past, the Present, and the Future!' (p. 81)?

....

....

....

....

b) What effect is conveyed by Scrooge's struggle to get dressed, for example putting things inside out and upside down?

....

....

....

....

c) Why does it matter that Scrooge does not send word to the Cratchits that the poultry is from him?

....

....

....

....

EXAM PREPARATION: WRITING ABOUT SCROOGE'S TRANSFORMATION (A01)

Read from *'I don't know what to do!'* (p. 81) to *'Oh glorious. Glorious!'* (p. 82)

Question: How does Dickens convey Scrooge's transformation in this scene?

Think about:

- What Scrooge does and says
- How Dickens creates atmosphere

3 Complete this table:

Point/detail	Evidence	Effect or explanation
1: *Scrooge acts strangely, showing confusion and uncertainty.*	*'laughing and crying in the same breath'*	*This is completely unlike his behaviour at the start of the novella, when he is very certain in his views.*
2: *Scrooge uses language which shows he is ready for a new beginning.*		
3: *Dickens uses similar language tecÚiques in Scrooge's speech and in his narration.*		

4 Write up **point 1** into a **paragraph** below in your own words. Remember to include what you infer from the evidence, or the writer's effects:

....

....

....

....

....

....

5 Now, choose **one** of your **other points** and write it out as another **paragraph** here:

....

....

....

....

....

....

....

....

PROGRESS LOG [tick the correct box]   Needs more work ☐   Getting there ☐   Under control ☐

Stave Five, pages 85–8: Fred and the Cratchits

QUICK TEST ✓

1 Complete this **gap-fill** quotation from the end of the novella, adding the **correct word or phrase**:

'Scrooge was better than his word. He did it all, and .... more; and to Tiny Tim, who did NOT die, he was a second .... He became as good a friend, as good a ...., and as good a man, as the .... old city knew, or any other .... old city, town or borough, in the .... old world. Some people laughed to see the alteration in him, but he let them laugh, and little heeded them; for he was .... enough to know that nothing ever happened on this globe, for good, at which some people did not have their fill of .... in the outset.'

THINKING MORE DEEPLY ❓

2 Write **one** or **two sentences** in response to each of these questions:

a) Why do you think Fred welcomes Scrooge without questioning why he has changed his mind about joining them?

....

....

....

....

....

b) Why does Bob want to call for 'help and a strait-waistcoat'?

....

....

....

....

....

c) Why do you think Dickens ends with the narrator's voice rather than a scene with Scrooge?

....

....

....

....

EXAM PREPARATION: WRITING ABOUT THE NARRATOR

A02

Read from *'Dear heart alive'* to *'overtake nine o' clock.'* (p. 86)

Question: What is the role of the intrusive narrator in this final scene?

Think about:

- What the narrator comments on
- The language used by the narrator

3 Complete this table:

Point/detail	Evidence	Effect or explanation
1: *The narrator first comments on Scrooge's niece.*	*'Dear heart alive, how his niece by marriage started!'*	*The narrator's use of exclamatory language echoes Fred's wife's shocked reaction, and adds impact. At the same time, the phrase 'Dear heart alive' is very gentle and offers connotations of warmth and even love.*
2: *Sometimes the narrator's language echoes Scrooge's thought patterns.*		
3: *The narrator is the storyteller but may also represent the reader: an ordinary person responding to this extraordinary tale.*		

4 Write up **point 1** into a **paragraph** below in your own words. Remember to include what you infer from the evidence, or the writer's effects:

....

....

....

....

....

5 Now, choose **one** of your **other points** and write it out as another **paragraph** here:

....

....

....

....

....

....

....

PROGRESS LOG [tick the correct box]   Needs more work ☐   Getting there ☐   Under control ☐

Practice task

1 First, **read** this **exam-style** task:

> Read the first three paragraphs of the novella, from: *'Marley was dead: to begin with.'* to *'solemnised it with an undoubted bargain.'* (p. 1)
>
> Question: Which aspects of the novella does Dickens set up in this opening passage?

2 Begin by circling the **key words** in the **question** above.

3 Now complete the table, noting down **3–4 key points** with **evidence** and the **effect** created:

Point	Evidence/quotation	Effect or explanation

4 **Draft your response.** Use the space below for your first paragraph(s) and then continue onto a sheet of paper:

Start: *In this extract, Dickens introduces various aspects of the novella which will become important. Firstly, ...* ....

....

....

....

....

....

....

....

....

....

....

PROGRESS LOG [tick the correct box]   Needs more work ☐   Getting there ☐   Under control ☐

Who's who?

Look at these drawings and **write** the **name** of each of the characters shown:

a) ....

b) F ....

c) ....

d) ....

e) I .... and

W...

f) ....

g) ....

h) F ....

l) B ....

j) B ....

k) ....

l) Mr F ....

Marley's Ghost

1 Each of the **character traits** below can be applied to Marley and/or his Ghost. **Working from memory**, identify whether these are more prominent during **his life or as a Ghost**. Then, still working from memory **add the point in the novella** when you think these are shown. Finally, add in a **quotation** from the novella:

Quality	In life or as Ghost?	Moment(s) in novella	Quotation
An excellent businessman			
Keen to help Scrooge			
Greedy			
Remorseful			

2 Using your **own judgement**, enter **evidence** from the novella on either side of the scales to weigh up whether the **influence** of Marley's Ghost on Scrooge is **negative** or **positive**.

The Ghost terrifies Scrooge

Scrooge's fear makes him obey

negative   positive

PROGRESS LOG [tick the correct box]   Needs more work ☐   Getting there ☐   Under control ☐

Ebenezer Scrooge

1 Using your **own judgement**, plot Scrooge's transformation through the novella by choosing **six key moments** to enter onto the graph **below**:

a) 'If they had rather die … they had better do it, and decrease the surplus population.' **(p.18)**

b) ....
....
....

c) ....
....
....

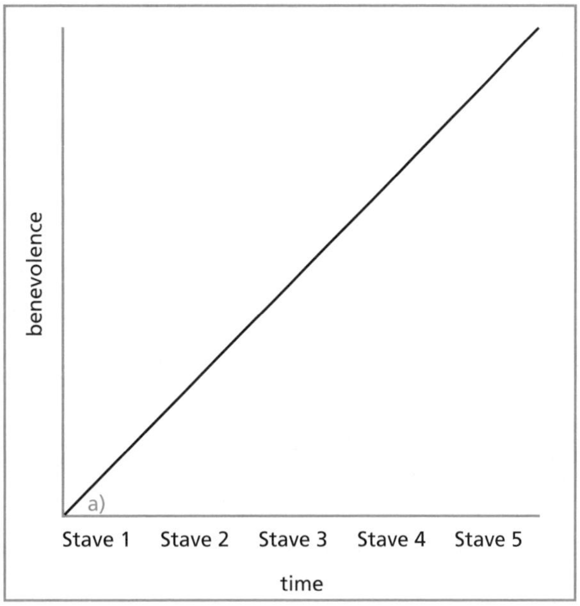

[Graph: vertical axis labelled "benevolence", horizontal axis labelled "time" with points Stave 1, Stave 2, Stave 3, Stave 4, Stave 5. A diagonal line rises from a) at bottom left to top right.]

d) ....
....
....

e) ....
....
....

f) ....
....
....

2 Look at this **quotation** about Scrooge. Add **annotations** to it by finding suitable adjectives from the bank below to explain how Dickens's words help to convey Scrooge's character:

avaricious = focused on acquiring material possessions

A squeezing, wrenching, grasping, scraping, clutching, <u>covetous old sinner</u>! Hard and sharp as flint, from which no steel had ever struck out generous fire; secret, and self-contained, and solitary as an oyster. The cold within him froze his old features, nipped his pointed nose, shrivelled his cheek, stiffened his gait; made his eyes red, his thin lips blue; and spoke out shrewdly in his grating voice. **(p. 2)**

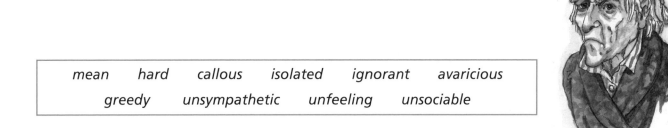

mean	*hard*	*callous*	*isolated*	*ignorant*	*avaricious*
greedy	*unsympathetic*	*unfeeling*	*unsociable*		

PROGRESS LOG [tick the correct box]   Needs more work ☐   Getting there ☐   Under control ☐

Fred

1 Look at the bank of **adjectives** describing Fred. **Circle** the ones you think best describe him:

optimistic	playful	jolly	kind	generous
spoilt	loving	respectful	cruel	affectionate
	cheerful	forgiving	ignorant	

2 Now add a **page reference** from your copy of the book next to each circle, showing where evidence can be found to support the adjective.

Bob Cratchit

1 Look at this **quotation** about Bob. Add further **annotations** to it by finding suitable adjectives from the bank below and explaining how Dickens's words help to convey Bob's character:

considerate = he thinks
of others' feelings

Bob was very cheerful with them, and spoke pleasantly to all the family. He looked at the work upon the table, and praised the industry and speed of Mrs Cratchit and the girls. They would be done long before Sunday, he said.

'Sunday! You went to-day then, Robert?' said his wife.

'Yes, my dear,' returned Bob. 'I wish you could have gone. It would have done you good to see how green a place it is. **(p. 77)**

gentle	loving	money-pinching	considerate	hardworking
fatherly	tired	humorous	timid	selfish	deferential	attentive

PROGRESS LOG [tick the correct box]   Needs more work ☐   Getting there ☐   Under control ☐

The Ghosts of Christmas

1 **Complete** the table below to help you **compare** the three Ghosts. Do as much as you can **from memory** in one colour pen. Then **check** in your copy of the novella and add more **detail** in a different colour:

	Physical attributes	Effect on and interaction with Scrooge	Attitude to and interaction with others
The Ghost of Christmas Past			
The Ghost of Christmas Present			
The Ghost of Christmas Yet to Come			

2 Write **two** or **three** sentences in answer to these questions:

a) How does Dickens imply that his Ghosts of Christmas have religious implications?

....

....

....

....

b) How does Dickens use symbolism in his Ghosts of Christmas?

....

....

....

....

....

PROGRESS LOG [tick the correct box]   Needs more work ☐   Getting there ☐   Under control ☐

Practice task

① First, **read** this **exam-style** task:

> Question: How does Dickens present and use the character of Bob Cratchit in the novella?

② Begin by circling the **key words** in the **question** above.

③ Now complete the table, noting down **3–4 key points** with **evidence** and the **effect** created:

Point	Evidence/quotation	Effect or explanation

④ **Draft your response**. Use the space below for your first paragraph(s) and then continue onto a sheet of paper:

Start: *Dickens uses the character of Bob Cratchit ...*

Themes

> **QUICK TEST** ✔

1 These **quotations** all relate to different **themes** in the novella. From the list below, match the best **abstract noun** to identify the **theme** in each case:

a) Marley's Ghost: 'Mankind was my business.' **(p. 18)**

b) Ghost of Christmas Present: 'most of all beware this boy, for on his brow I see that written which is Doom' **(p. 63)**

c) One of the 'portly gentlemen': 'it is a time, of all others, when Want is keenly felt, and Abundance rejoices' **(p. 7)**

d) Marley's Ghost: 'I have sat invisible beside you many and many a day.' **(p. 18)**

e) 'Scrooge sat down upon a form, and wept to see his poor forgotten self as he had used to be.' **(p. 27)**

education	*isolation*	*poverty*
responsibility	*the supernatural*	

2 Complete this **gap-fill paragraph** about the **theme** of **happiness**, adding the **correct or suitable** information:

As well as using his novella to show how it is morally .... to assume the poor are inadequate or lazy, Dickens also uses his characters to show that .... does not automatically bring happiness. The characters in 'A Christmas Carol' who are happy are clearly shown to be so by their ...., not because of material wealth. Both Fred and Bob love their families and are happy, but materially and in terms of social .... they are very different. Dickens therefore does not wish his readers to conclude that it is Fred's .... which enables him to be happy, as otherwise Bob could not also show a .... positive outlook.

> **PROGRESS LOG** [tick the correct box]   Needs more work ☐   Getting there ☐   Under control ☐

THINKING MORE DEEPLY

?

3 Write one or two sentences to show how these comments relay Dickens's message about generosity:

a) Of Mr Fezziwig's party: 'In came the boy from over the way, who was suspected of not having board enough from his master.' **(p. 32)**

....

....

....

....

b) The Ghost of Christmas Present: '"Why to a poor one most?" asked Scrooge. "Because it needs it most"' **(p. 46)**

....

....

....

....

c) 'He [Tiny Tim] told me, coming home, that he hoped the people saw him in the church, because he was a cripple, and it might be pleasant to them to remember upon Christmas Day, who made lame beggars walk and blind men see.' **(p. 49)**

....

....

....

....

4 Complete each statement about the theme of isolation:

a) *Scrooge seems happy to be alone at the start of the story. However, this is not*

the case when ... .

....

....

b) *Dickens suggests that the effects of isolation ...* ....

....

....

c) *Scrooge is transformed in terms of the theme of isolation ...* ....

....

....

....

PROGRESS LOG [tick the correct box]   Needs more work ☐   Getting there ☐   Under control ☐

EXAM PREPARATION: WRITING ABOUT REDEMPTION

Read from *'Scrooge fell upon his knees'* (p. 16) to the end of Stave One (p. 20).

Question: How does Dickens present the theme of redemption through Marley's offer to Scrooge?

Think about:

- What Marley says to Scrooge
- What Marley shows to Scrooge

5 Complete this table:

Point/detail	Evidence	Effect or explanation
1: *Marley explains that Spirits must make up for what they failed to do in life.*	*'condemned to do so after death'*	*This sets up the idea that Scrooge would have something to make up for and therefore needs redemption.*
2: *Marley shows Scrooge his chains and makes Scrooge believe that his would be even longer and heavier.*		
3: *Marley shows Scrooge a host of Spirits filling the night air.*		

6 Write up **point 1** into a **paragraph** below in your own words. Remember to include what you infer from the evidence, or the writer's effects:

....

....

....

....

....

....

7 Now, choose **one** of your **other points** and write it out as another **paragraph** here:

....

....

....

....

....

....

....

....

PROGRESS LOG [tick the correct box]   Needs more work ☐   Getting there ☐   Under control ☐

Contexts

QUICK TEST ✔

1 Which of these are **TRUE** statements about the contexts of this novella, and which are **FALSE**? Write 'T' or 'F' in the boxes:

a) Dickens disapproved of the 1834 Poor Laws, because he thought they did not do enough to protect poor people. ☐

b) The workhouse that Scrooge refers to was a place where the poor could be housed and fed while they looked for suitable work. ☐

c) Many of the practices for celebrating Christmas described by Dickens in the novella have since become well-established traditions because of the story. ☐

d) The Industrial Revolution brought many people from the countryside into the cities, where they all became very wealthy factory workers. ☐

e) Dickens uses broad Christian-influenced morality rather than strict Church teachings to inform the morals of this story. ☐

2 Circle the correct answer about the **context** of the novella to **finish the statement**:

a) Dickens makes Scrooge visit [London / the countryside / the countryside and London].

b) The 'portly gentlemen' visit Scrooge in order to express Dickens's views about [the Poor Laws / Christmas / wealth].

c) Dickens's childhood experience of working in a [mill / blacking factory / stable] informs the novella.

d) The scenes of Scrooge being isolated as a child may also have drawn on Dickens's childhood, because his father and seven of his siblings went to [the workhouse / another town to find work / a debtors' prison], leaving the young Charles to look after himself.

> **THINKING MORE DEEPLY** **(?)**

3 Write **one** or **two sentences** in response to each of these questions:

a) How does Dickens show us that the Cratchits are poor?

....

....

....

....

....

b) What impression do we have of how typical Scrooge's views are?

....

....

....

....

4 How effective do you think *A Christmas Carol* would be in **persuading** readers of the time to **think differently** about how the poor were treated? Using your **own judgement**, **complete** this table with ideas **FOR** and **AGAINST** using a story in the way Dickens has here:

FOR: This would be an effective way of persuading Victorian readers		AGAINST: This would not be an effective way of persuading Victorian readers	
Point	Evidence	Point	Evidence

PROGRESS LOG [tick the correct box]   Needs more work ☐   Getting there ☐   Under control ☐

Settings

1 For each of these London settings, write down a **significant event** from the novella:

a)

Fred's house

....

....

....

b)

Scrooge's house

....

....

....

c)

Scrooge's grave

....

....

....

d)

Scrooge's office

....

....

....

e)

Joe's shop

....

....

....

f)

The Cratchits' house

....

....

....

THINKING MORE DEEPLY   **?**

2 Write **two** or **three sentences** in response to each of these questions:

a) What do Dickens's descriptions of happy homes (Belle's family, the Cratchit family, Fred's family) have in common?

....

....

....

....

....

b) How does Dickens use the weather as a setting in this novella?

....

....

....

....

....

3 The Ghost of Christmas Present takes Scrooge to some **isolated** locations. Use your **own judgement** and the **table** below to **compare** the description of these isolated places with **either** the **schoolhouse** in Stave Three **or** the site of **Scrooge's grave** in Stave Four:

Location visited	Description	Comparison with school house or Scrooge's grave
Moorland		
Rocks with a lighthouse		
Out to sea		

PROGRESS LOG [tick the correct box]   Needs more work ☐   Getting there ☐   Under control ☐

Practice task

1 First, **read** this **exam-style** task:

Question: Choose three characters from *A Christmas Carol* and describe their attitude to the theme of responsibility.

2 Begin by circling the **key words** in the **question** above.

3 Now complete the table, noting down **3–4 key points** with **evidence** and the **effect** created:

Character/attitude	Evidence/quotation	Effect or explanation

4 **Draft your response**. Use the space below for your first paragraph(s) and then continue onto a sheet of paper:

Start: *The three characters I wish to discuss all show differing attitudes to the concept of responsibility. For example …* ....

....

....

....

....

....

....

....

....

....

PROGRESS LOG [tick the correct box]   Needs more work ☐   Getting there ☐   Under control ☐

PART FIVE: FORM, STRUCTURE AND LANGUAGE

Form

QUICK TEST ✔

1 Complete this **gap-fill paragraph** about the form of the novella, with the **correct** or **suitable** information:

'A Christmas Carol' is written to evoke the fireside tales format, and specifically that

of a .... story. Dickens uses .... instead of chapters, perhaps to

show that he is .... or playing with form, rather than writing a serious story.

He wanted this story to be heard by many people, because its core ....

was very important to him. In keeping with the ghost story form, Dickens uses an

.... narrator who often comments on the action and reminds us that we are

listening to (or reading) a story. This form also allows him to write in a ....

and sometimes .... way, as well as making some things possible that would

otherwise be .... Finally, the moral message is delivered in a ....

way, with a threat of eternal punishment, and yet the message is given with warmth

and ....

THINKING MORE DEEPLY ?

2 Write **one** or **two sentences** in response to each of these questions:

a) Apart from the existence of the Ghosts, which aspects of the story would be difficult to achieve in a more realistic way?

....

....

....

....

....

b) What is a novella and how does Dickens use the form?

....

....

....

....

....

PROGRESS LOG [tick the correct box]   Needs more work ☐   Getting there ☐   Under control ☐

Structure

QUICK TEST ✓

1 **Circle** the correct answer about the novella's **structure** to **complete the statement**:

a) Marley's Ghost's appearance is the [reversal / precipitating incident / rising action].

b) The Ghosts of Christmas create the [reversal / precipitating incident / rising action].

c) The moment when Scrooge's gravestone is revealed is the plot's [climax / epiphany / resolution].

d) Scrooge's vow to 'honour Christmas in my heart, and try to keep it all the year' (p. 80) is the story's moment of [climax / epiphany / resolution].

e) Dickens uses a [standard / unusual / complex] structure in *A Christmas Carol* in order to help the audience to focus on his message.

THINKING MORE DEEPLY ?

2 Enter **evidence** from Staves **One** and **Five** on either side of the scales to show how Dickens makes Scrooge's **actions** at the start and end of the novella **balance out**. Find evidence of how Scrooge behaves in Staves One and Five with:

- The portly gentlemen

  ....
  ....
  ....

- Fred

  ....
  ....
  ....

- Bob

  ....
  ....
  ....

Stave One   **Stave Five**

- The portly gentlemen

  ....
  ....
  ....

- Fred

  ....
  ....
  ....

- Bob

  ....
  ....
  ....

EXAM PREPARATION: WRITING ABOUT FORESHADOWING A02

Read Stave One from the beginning to *'astonish his son's weak mind.'* (p. 2)

Question: How does Dickens control the reader's expectations about the story?

Think about:

- What the narrator explains and how
- What the reader is encouraged to focus on

3 Complete this table:

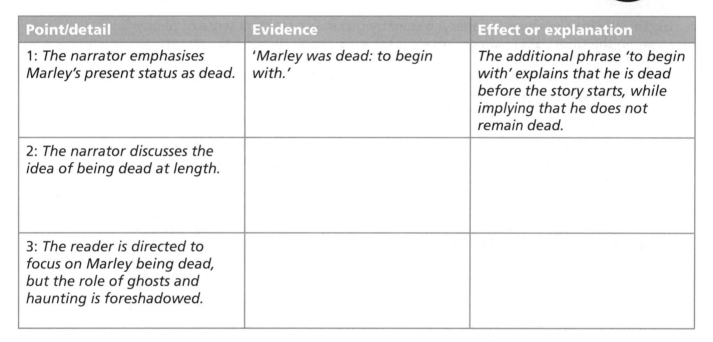

Point/detail	Evidence	Effect or explanation
1: *The narrator emphasises Marley's present status as dead.*	*'Marley was dead: to begin with.'*	*The additional phrase 'to begin with' explains that he is dead before the story starts, while implying that he does not remain dead.*
2: *The narrator discusses the idea of being dead at length.*		
3: *The reader is directed to focus on Marley being dead, but the role of ghosts and haunting is foreshadowed.*		

4 Write up **point 1** into a **paragraph** below in your own words. Remember to include what you infer from the evidence, or the writer's effects:

....

....

....

....

....

5 Now, choose **one** of your **other points** and write it out as another **paragraph** here:

....

....

....

....

....

....

....

PROGRESS LOG [tick the correct box] Needs more work ☐ Getting there ☐ Under control ☐

Language

QUICK TEST ✔

1 **Circle** the correct **linguistic or literary term** to **complete the statement**:

a) Dickens uses the [metaphor / simile / personification] 'solitary as an oyster' (p. 2) to show how closed-up and isolated Scrooge is, but also to hint that there is something valuable inside him.

b) [Listing / Rule of three / Imagery] is used by Dickens to create a sense of plenty when the Ghost of Christmas Present is taking Scrooge through the streets.

c) Dickens uses the [noun / adverb / adjective] 'tremulous' to show how Bob's voice wavers when he speaks about Tiny Tim.

d) Dickens uses the [simile / personification / adjective] of 'potatoes bubbling up, knocked loudly at the saucepan-lid to be let out and peeled' (p. 48) as an example of the excitement in the Cratchit household: even the dinner is affected.

e) Dickens uses the [noun / adjective / adverb] 'timidly' in the clause 'Scrooge entered timidly' (p. 42) to indicate that Scrooge has already begun to change a little because he is showing respect to the Ghost of Christmas Present.

THINKING MORE DEEPLY ?

2 Write **two** or **three sentences** in response to each of these questions:

a) Why do you think Dickens uses so much weather imagery in setting up the story?

....
....
....
....
....
....
....

b) How does Dickens develop Scrooge's bed as a symbol in the novella?

....
....
....
....
....
....
....
....

THINKING MORE DEEPLY ?

❸ **Complete** this **table** by selecting three **significant** moments of **intrusive narration** and adding a quotation and analysis for each:

Intrusive narration	Quotation	Analysis or explanation
1: *Dickens uses the intrusive narrator to conform to the fireside ghost story genre.*		
2: *Dickens uses the intrusive narrator to make judgemental comments about Scrooge.*		
3: *Dickens uses the intrusive narrator to help the audience understand more than Scrooge.*		

❹ Look at this **quotation** from Marley's Ghost. Add further **annotations** to it by finding suitable terms from the bank at the bottom of the page and explaining how Dickens uses these features to create impact:

repetition = emphasises routine and habit

'I wear the chain I forged in life … I made it <u>link by link, and yard by yard</u>; I girded it on of my own free will, and of my own free will I wore it.'

conjunction	adjective	pronoun	repetition
symbol	verb	imagery	

PROGRESS LOG [tick the correct box]   Needs more work ☐   Getting there ☐   Under control ☐

EXAM PREPARATION: WRITING ABOUT THE NEW SCROOGE · A02

Read the beginning of Stave Five from *'Yes! And the bedpost was his own.'* to *'every kind of extravagance.'* (p. 81)

Question: How does Dickens use language to evoke Scrooge's transformation?

Think about:

● The way events are narrated

● The way Scrooge speaks

5 Complete this table:

TecÚique	Evidence	Effect or explanation
1: *Short sentences*	*'Yes! And the bedpost was his own.'*	*These reveal his straightforward thought processes as he celebrates being returned safely.*
2: *Repetition and near-repetition*		
3: *Lists*		

6 Write up **point 1** into a **paragraph** below in your own words. Remember to include what you infer from the evidence, or the writer's effects:

....

....

....

....

....

....

7 Now, choose **one** of your **other points** and write it out as another **paragraph** here:

....

....

....

....

....

....

....

PROGRESS LOG [tick the correct box]   Needs more work ☐   Getting there ☐   Under control ☐

Practice task

1 First, **read** this **exam-style** task:

> Question: To what extent is *A Christmas Carol* a simple ghost story?

2 Begin by circling the **key words** in the **question** above.

3 Now complete the table, noting down **3–4 key points** with **evidence** and the **effect** created:

Point	Evidence/quotation	Effect or explanation

4 **Draft your response.** Use the space below for your first paragraph(s) and then continue onto a sheet of paper:

Start: *'A Christmas Carol' can be said to be a ghost story in that …* ....

....

....

....

....

....

....

....

....

....

....

....

....

PROGRESS LOG [tick the correct box]   Needs more work ☐   Getting there ☐   Under control ☐

PART SIX: Progress Booster

Expressing and explaining ideas

1 How well can you express your ideas about *A Christmas Carol*? Look at this grid and tick the level you think you are currently at:

Level	How you respond	Writing skills	Tick
High	• You analyse the effect of specific words and phrases very closely (i.e. 'zooming in' on them and exploring their meaning). • You select quotations very carefully and you embed them fluently in your sentences. • You are persuasive and convincing in the points you make, often coming up with original ideas.	You use a wide range of specialist terms (words like 'imagery'), excellent punctuation, accurate spelling, grammar, etc.	
Mid/ Good	• You analyse some parts of the text closely, but not all the time. • You support what you say with evidence and quotations, but sometimes your writing could be more fluent to read. • You make relevant comments on the text.	You use a good range of specialist terms, generally accurate punctuation, usually accurate spelling, grammar, etc.	
Lower	• You comment on some words and phrases but often you do not develop your ideas. • You sometimes use quotations to back up what you say but they are not always well chosen. • You mention the effect of certain words and phrases but these are not always relevant to the task.	You do not have a very wide range of specialist terms, but you have reasonably accurate spelling, punctuation and grammar.	

SELECTING AND USING QUOTATIONS

2 Read these two samples from students' responses to a question about how the intrusive narrator is presented. Decide which of the three levels they fit best, i.e. **lower (L)**, **mid (M)** or **high (H)**:

Student A: *The intrusive narrator addresses the audience directly when Scrooge is waiting for the second spirit. Scrooge's anticipation is introduced with 'I don't mind calling on you to believe that …', which shows the narrator's personality and reminds us that we are being told a story.*

Level? ☐   Why? ....

....

....

Student B: *Dickens brings the intrusive narrator in while Scrooge is waiting for the second spirit. The narrator uses pronouns to tell us 'I don't mind calling on you …', as though he is present with us, telling us the story personally. This prevents readers from being too caught up in the story, making them more likely to listen to Dickens's moral message.*

Level? ☐   Why? ....

....

....

ZOOMING IN – YOUR TURN!

Here is the first part of another student response. The student has picked a good quotation but he hasn't 'zoomed in' on any particular words or phrases:

Dickens creates a vivid atmosphere through his depictions of the weather in Stave One, e.g. 'The ancient tower of a church ... became invisible, and struck the hours and quarters in the clouds, with tremulous vibrations afterwards, as if its teeth were chattering in its frozen head up there.'

3 Pick out one of the **words** or **phrases** the student has quoted and write a further sentence to complete the explanation:

The word/phrase ' .... *' suggests* ....

....

....

EXPLAINING IDEAS

You need to be precise about the way Dickens gets ideas across. This can be done by varying your use of verbs (not just using 'says' or 'means').

4 Read this paragraph from a **mid-level** response to a question about Scrooge's initial attitude to the poor. Circle all the **verbs** that are repeated (not in the quotations):

Dickens shows Scrooge's absolute inability to have empathy for the poor through the climax to his conversation with the 'portly gentlemen'. When Scrooge says that they should 'decrease the surplus population' by dying, this not only shows his lack of understanding, but it also says that he sees them as less than human, since he shows no human feeling for them at all.

5 Now choose some of the words below to replace your circled ones:

suggests	implies	tells us	presents	signals	asks	demonstrates
recognise	comprehend	reveals	conveys	indicates	states	portrays

6 Rewrite your **high-level** version of the paragraph in full below. Remember to mention the **author by name** to show you understand he is **making choices** in how he presents characters, themes and events:

....

....

....

....

....

....

....

PROGRESS LOG [tick the correct box]　　Needs more work ☐　　Getting there ☐　　Under control ☐

Making inferences and interpretations (A02)

WRITING ABOUT INFERENCES

You need to be able to show that you can read between the lines, and make inferences, rather than just explain more explicit 'surface' meanings.

Here is an extract from one student's **high-level** response to a question about Scrooge and how he is presented:

Towards the end of Stave Four, Scrooge wants to see 'what I shall be, in days to come'. This reveals Scrooge's lack of understanding of the process he is undergoing: he feels that he has already changed and, therefore, that the vision of himself in the future will reflect this change. This suggests that he has not understood that the process which Marley set in motion for his redemption has not yet been completed, and he has some way to go before his future self can be saved.

1 Look at the response carefully:

- **Underline** the simple point which explains what Scrooge thinks.
- **Circle** the sentence that develops the first point.
- **Highlight** the sentence that shows an inference and begins to explore wider interpretations.

INTERPRETING – YOUR TURN!

2 Read the opening to this student response carefully and then **choose the point** from a), b) or c) which shows **inference** and could lead to **a deeper interpretation**. Remember – interpreting is *not* guesswork!

Mr Fezziwig acts as a foil to Scrooge because he behaves with responsibility towards his employees and others around him. Scrooge clearly understands this when he says 'He has the power to render us happy or unhappy'. This shows that Scrooge recognises why Mr Fezziwig is so popular. It also suggests that …

a) … Fezziwig's behaviour affects how people feel.

b) … Scrooge is beginning to understand his own responsibility and the effect his actions have on others.

c) … he knows that people like Mr Fezziwig are in powerful positions.

3 Now **complete** this **paragraph** about Bob, adding your own final sentence which makes inferences or explores wider interpretations:

Bob is presented as a sympathetic character who has put up with a great deal working for Scrooge. When Dickens shows him with his family, he is described as 'little Bob, the father … his threadbare clothes darned up and brushed, to look seasonable; and Tiny Tim upon his shoulder'. This suggests that … ....

....

....

....

| PROGRESS LOG [tick the correct box] | Needs more work ☐ | Getting there ☐ | Under control ☐ |

Writing about context (A03)

When you write about context you must make sure that what you write is relevant to the task.

Read this comment by a student about Scrooge:

Scrooge's social position, along with his attitude to keeping his wealth, are both evident in Dickens's descriptions of his home in Stave One. Many rooms are listed, 'Sitting room, bed-room, lumber-room', which sounds quite grand for the Victorian context, but the furnishings appear relatively poor in contrast and he has a 'little saucepan of gruel' to eat. This contrast reveals his meanness and desire to hold onto his money rather than spend it, even on himself.

❶ Why is this an **effective paragraph** about **context**? Select a), b) or c):

   a) It explains Scrooge's meanness.

   b) It makes the link between Scrooge's home at this time and his character.

   c) It tells us what some houses were like in the nineteenth century.

YOUR TURN!

❷ Now read this **further paragraph**, and complete it by **choosing a suitable point** from a), b) or c) related to context:

Attitudes to the poor in the novella reflect some contemporary social attitudes that Dickens wanted to highlight. Scrooge holds negative beliefs about the poor, and Dickens uses Scrooge to make clear that his views are not acceptable. His objectionable opinions can be seen when he says …

   a) *'And the Union workhouses?' demanded Scrooge. 'Are they still in operation?'* This shows his firm belief in government policy and Malthusian economic theory.

   b) *'But you were always a good man of business, Jacob'.* This shows that he thinks being a good business man is important.

   c) *'Spirit!' said Scrooge, 'show me no more!'* This shows that he cannot bear to see the truth of poverty.

❸ Now, starting here and continuing onto a separate sheet of paper, **write a paragraph** about how Dickens uses the context of poverty in the Victorian period to describe the Cratchits' home and life:

....

....

....

....

PROGRESS LOG [tick the correct box]   Needs more work ☐   Getting there ☐   Under control ☐

Structure and linking of paragraphs

Paragraphs need to demonstrate your points clearly by:

- Using **topic sentences**
- Focusing on **key words** from quotations
- Explaining their **effect** or meaning

1 Read this model paragraph in which a student explains how Dickens presents the Ghosts:

Dickens presents the Ghosts as guides who help Scrooge learn from the scenes he is shown. They sometimes highlight his previous bad behaviour in order to do this, for example, repeating Scrooge's words back to him and calling him an 'Insect'. This teaches Scrooge how insignificant he is and demonstrates to him that he does not have the right to judge or criticise others.

Look at the response carefully:

- **Underline** the topic sentence which explains the main point about the Ghosts.
- **Circle** the word that the Ghosts use to describe Scrooge.
- **Highlight** the part of the last sentence which explains the word.

2 Now read this paragraph by a student who is explaining how Dickens presents Fred:

We learn more about Fred when he is talking to his family about Scrooge: 'He may rail at Christmas till he dies, but he can't help thinking better of it – I defy him – if he finds me going there, in good temper, year after year, and saying Uncle Scrooge, how are you?' This tells us what kind of person Fred is.

Expert viewpoint: This paragraph is unclear. It does not begin with a topic sentence to explain how Dickens presents Fred and does not zoom in on any key words that tell us what Fred is like.

Now **rewrite the paragraph**. Start with a **topic sentence**, and pick out a **key word or phrase** to 'zoom in' on, then follow up with an **explanation** or **interpretation**:

Dickens presents Fred as ....

....

....

....

....

....

....

....

....

....

....

....

It is equally important to make your **sentences link together** and your **ideas follow on** fluently from each other. You can do this by:

● Using a mixture of short and long sentences as appropriate

● Using words or phrases that help connect or develop ideas

❸ Read this model paragraph by one student writing about Scrooge and how he is presented:

Dickens presents Scrooge as an older man who seems very set in his ways. At the start of the novella, his ideas about Christmas and other people appear very fixed, for example when he refuses to help 'Idle people', suggesting that he has no sympathy for the poor whatsoever. By the end of the novella, he is transformed. The insights the Ghosts give him into other people's lives make it impossible for him to continue to dehumanise them, which changes his outlook completely.

Look at the response carefully:

● Underline the topic sentence which introduces the main idea.

● Underline the short sentence which signals a change in ideas.

● Circle any words or phrases that link ideas such as 'who', 'when', 'implying', 'which', etc.

❹ Read this paragraph by another student also commenting on how Scrooge is presented:

Dickens creates a clear image of some aspects of Scrooge's appearance. This is found in Stave One. He is described as 'his eyes red, his thin lips blue' and 'A frosty rime was on his head, and on his eyebrows, and his wiry chin.' All this is because he has his own 'cold within him'. This suggests what an uncaring and callous man he is. He always makes everywhere cold because he is such an unfeeling person.

Expert viewpoint: The candidate has understood how the character's nature is revealed in his appearance. However, the paragraph is rather awkwardly written. It needs improving by linking the sentences with suitable phrases and joining words such as: 'where', 'in', 'as well as', 'who', 'suggesting', 'implying'.

Rewrite the **paragraph**, improving the **style**, and also try to add a **concluding sentence** summing up Scrooge's character and appearance.

Start with the same **topic sentence**, but extend it:

Dickens creates a clear image of some aspects of Scrooge's appearance ... .

....

....

....

....

....

....

....

....

PROGRESS LOG [tick the correct box]   Needs more work ☐   Getting there ☐   Under control ☐

Writing skills

Here are a number of key words you might use when writing in the exam:

Content and structure	Characters and style	Linguistic features
stave	character	metaphor
scene	role	personification
quotation	protagonist	juxtaposition
sequence	dramatic	dramatic irony
dialogue	supernatural	repetition
climax	villainous	symbol
development	humorous	foreshadowing
description	sympathetic	euphemism

1 **Circle** any you might find difficult to spell, and then use the 'Look, Say, Cover, Write, Check' method to learn them. This means: **look** at the word; **say** it out loud; then **cover** it up; **write** it out; uncover and **check** your spelling with the correct version.

2 Create a **mnemonic** for five of your difficult spellings. For example:

symbol: **s**even **y**oung **m**en **b**ounced **o**ver London

Or

break the word down: SYM – BOL!

a) ....

b) ....

c) ....

d) ....

e) ....

3 **Circle** any **incorrect spellings** in this paragraph and then rewrite it:

At the begginning of Stave Two, Dickens builds the tention rappidly as Scrooge cannot beleve the time from his 'prepostorous little clock'. The uncertenty created about the time makes the audiense unsure about what is hapening and how the ghostes are controling Scrooge's world. This techniqe makes the audiense sympathyse with Scrooge as we feel the same as him.

....

....

....

....

....

....

Punctuation can help make your meaning clear.

Here is one response by a student commenting on the intrusive narrator that Dickens uses in *A Christmas Carol*. Check for correct use of:

- Apostrophes
- Speech marks for quotations and emphasis
- Full stops, commas and capital letters

Dicken's use of an Intrusive Narrator in the novella often has the function of reminding, the audience that they are reading, or listening to, a story. It is there from the start eg scrooge and he were partners for i don't know how many years he may have done this to help emphasise his moral message, about caring for 'others'.

4 **Rewrite** it **correctly** here:

....
....
....
....
....
....

5 It is better to use the **present tense** to describe what is happening in the novella.

Look at these two extracts. Which one uses tenses **consistently** and **accurately**?

Student A: *Dickens showed us Scrooge's gradual transformation from callous to benevolent. In Stave One, Scrooge believed that 'prisons' and 'workhouses' are the answers to the problems of the poor, while by the end of the novella, after the Ghosts' visits, he was 'as good a man' as it is possible to be.*

Student B: *Dickens shows us Scrooge's gradual transformation from callous to benevolent. In Stave One, Scrooge believes that 'prisons' and 'workhouses' are the answers to the problems of the poor, while by the end of the novella, after the Ghosts' visits, he is 'as good a man' as it is possible to be.*

6 Now look at this further paragraph. Underline or circle all the verb **tenses** first:

The Ghost of Christmas Present tried to teach Scrooge by calling him an 'Insect on the leaf' and comparing him to 'his hungry brothers in the dust'. With this metaphor of Scrooge 'on the leaf', Dickens implied that he was lucky to have enough to live on, while the word 'brothers' implicitly connects Scrooge and the poor.

Now **rewrite** it using the **present tense** consistently:

....
....
....
....
....
....

PROGRESS LOG [tick the correct box]   Needs more work ☐   Getting there ☐   Under control ☐

Tackling exam tasks   (A01)(A02)

DECODING QUESTIONS

It is important to be able to identify **key words** in exam tasks and then quickly generate some ideas.

Read this task and notice how the **key words** have been underlined:

Question: _In what ways_ does _Scrooge_ _respond_ to the _Ghosts_ _throughout the novella_?

Write about:

- How Scrooge responds to the Ghosts both <u>at the start</u>, and <u>as the novella progresses</u>
- How <u>Dickens presents Scrooge</u> by the <u>ways he writes</u>

1 Now do the same with this task, i.e. **underline** the **key words**:

Question: _How does Dickens tackle ideas about social class and poverty in the novella?_

Write about:

- How rich and poor people are discussed in the novella
- How Dickens presents the idea of helping the poor

GENERATING IDEAS

2 Now you need to generate ideas quickly. Use the spider-diagram* below and add as many ideas of your own as you can:

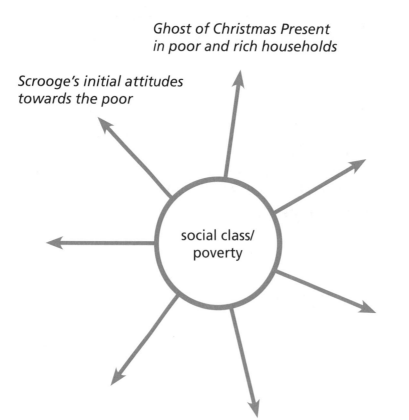

_Ghost of Christmas Present
in poor and rich households_

_Scrooge's initial attitudes
towards the poor_

social class/
poverty

*You can do this as a list if you wish.

PLANNING AN ESSAY

Here is the **exam-style** task from the previous page:

Question: *How does Dickens tackle ideas about social class and poverty in the novella?*

Write about:

- How rich and poor people are discussed in the novella
- How Dickens presents the idea of helping the poor

③ Using the ideas you generated, write a simple **plan** with at least **five key points** (the first two have been done for you). Check back to your spider diagram or the list you made:

a) *Dickens depicts Scrooge's callous attitude to the poor.*

b) *The Ghost of Christmas Present gives examples of the rich and the poor celebrating Christmas in similar ways.*

c) ....

d) ....

e) ....

④ Now list **five quotations** for each point (the first two have been provided for you):

a) *'If they had rather die,' said Scrooge, 'they had better do it, and decrease the surplus population.'*

b) *'Much they saw, and far they went, and many homes they visited, but always with a happy end.'*

c) ....

d) ....

e) ....

⑤ Now read this task and **write a plan** of your own, including **quotations**, on a separate sheet of paper:

Read from *'The cellar-door flew open with a booming sound'* (p. 13) to *'but he could see nothing.'* (p. 16)

Question: *How is the Ghost of Jacob Marley depicted in this scene and how does Scrooge respond to him?*

PROGRESS LOG [tick the correct box]   Needs more work ☐   Getting there ☐   Under control ☐

Sample answers (A01)(A02)(A03)

OPENING PARAGRAPHS

Look at this task:

Question: *How does Dickens present the theme of social responsibility in the novella?*

Now look at these two alternate openings to the essay and read the examiner comments underneath:

Student A

Dickens portrays the theme of social responsibility in different ways throughout the novella, ultimately attempting to steer his audience towards his views. We are clearly expected to view Scrooge's initial attitude negatively, when he refuses to contribute to the collection being taken around the offices. This theme is further developed through the Cratchits.

Student B

Scrooge shows a complete lack of social responsibility at the start of the novella. He is completely unwilling to give money to the charity collectors, instead thinking that the workhouse and the prisons are the right things to deal with the poor.

Expert viewpoint 1: This is a clear opening paragraph that introduces some of the ideas to be discussed and highlights the main idea, that Dickens is intending to share his views with the audience. The Cratchits' role in the theme needs to be developed further.

Mid level

Expert viewpoint 2: This opening recounts Scrooge's attitude to social responsibility, without outlining what is to be discussed in the essay, which is the point of the introduction. Other ways in which Dickens highlights issues of social responsibility also need to be mentioned.

Lower level

① Which comment belongs to which answer? Match the paragraph (A or B) to the expert's feedback (1 or 2).

Student A: ....   Student B: ....

② Now it's your turn. Write the opening paragraph to this task on a separate sheet of paper:

Read from *'The curtains of his bed were drawn aside'* (p. 23) to *'clasped its robe in supplication.'* (p. 25)

Question: *How is the Ghost depicted in this scene and how does Scrooge respond to him?*

Remember:

- Introduce the topic in general terms, perhaps **explaining** or '**unpicking**' the key **words** or **ideas** in the task (such as 'depict').

- Mention the **different possibilities** or ideas that you are going to address.

- Use the **author's name**.

> ## WRITING ABOUT TECHNIQUES

Here are two paragraphs in response to a different task, where the students have focused on the writer's techniques. The task is:

Read from: *'Then up rose Mrs Cratchit'* (p. 47) to *'limbs supported by an iron frame!'* (p. 48)

Question: *What techniques does Dickens use to evoke Christmas in the Cratchit household?*

Student A

Dickens shows the younger Cratchits bursting in, making their home seem noisy and busy. He says they are 'tearing in, screaming that outside the baker's they had smelt the goose and known it for their own'. This creates humour as they would not have been able to tell the smell of their goose from all the other people's at the baker's. This is a really vivid way of describing the family.

Student B

Dickens depicts the Cratchits with both affection and comedy in this scene, reinforcing their dual roles as light relief and representing the poor. The younger Cratchits' entrance is shown vividly with the verbs 'tearing in, screaming', which is then contrasted with their 'basking in luxurious thoughts of sage and onion'. Here Dickens invokes irony, as stuffing is not a luxury item, yet it seems so to the Cratchits. Their certainty that they had been able to identify the smell of their goose, conveyed by the rhyming phrase 'known it for their own', is also humorous and charming.

Expert viewpoint 1: This high-level response clearly describes some aspects of Christmas in the Cratchit household. It also discusses some techniques and sets these briefly in the context of the characters' roles in the text as a whole, using linguistic terms effectively. It would be useful to explain more about the Cratchits' roles in the novella but the paragraph overall is sound.

High level

Expert viewpoint 2: This mid-level response highlights some aspects of the Cratchits' home at Christmas. However, the quotation, though appropriate, is not sufficiently embedded in the sentence. There is one instance of the writer's technique mentioned but no others and the long quotation is explained broadly, with no detailed analysis.

Mid level

❸ Which comment belongs to which answer? Match the paragraph (A or B) to the expert's feedback (1 or 2).

Student A: ....   Student B: ....

❹ Now, take another **aspect** of the scene and on a separate sheet of paper write your own **paragraph**. You could **comment** on one of these aspects:

- Mrs Cratchit's clothing
- Martha's arrival
- The arrival of Bob and Tiny Tim

Now read this **lower-level** response to the following task:

Read from *'The cellar-door flew open with a booming sound'* (p. 13) to *'but he could see nothing.'* (p. 16)

Question: *How is the Ghost of Jacob Marley depicted in this scene and how does Scrooge respond to him?*

Student response:

> When Jacob Marley arrives in this passage, it is first shown by sound: 'a booming sound' and Dickens explains how Scrooge hears it getting closer and closer to him. At first Scrooge says he isn't bothered about it, calling it 'humbug', which is like saying it's a load of rubbish. Scrooge's 'colour changed' when the noise came into the room, though, so we know that he is scared really.
>
> It seems like even the fire recognises Marley, so we can see that Scrooge cannot get away with pretending not to know it's him.

Expert viewpoint: The first quotation in paragraph 1 is well chosen and it is a good point that Scrooge hears Marley before seeing him at this point, but the quotation is not effectively embedded in a sentence. Neither paragraph really explores the effect that Marley's Ghost has on Scrooge. The response needs to more clearly focus on what Dickens intends, and the language is often too informal, e.g. 'load of rubbish'.

⑤ Rewrite these two **paragraphs** in your own words, improving them by addressing:

- The lack of development of linking of points – no 'zooming in' on key words and phrases
- The lack of embedded quotations
- Unnecessary repetition, poor specialist terms and use of informal vocabulary

Paragraph 1:

In this scene, Dickens depicts Marley's Ghost as ....

....

and also ....

....

This implies that ....

....

Paragraph 2:

Scrooge's response to the Ghost is at first ....

....

However, ...

....

This links to ....

....

....

....

A FULL-LENGTH RESPONSE

6 Write a **full-length response** to this exam-style task on a separate sheet of paper. Answer **both parts** of the question:

> Question: *How is Fred depicted by Dickens throughout the novella?*
>
> Write about:
> - How Dickens presents Fred interacting with Scrooge directly
> - How Dickens presents Fred through what Scrooge is shown by the Ghosts

Remember to do the following:

- Plan **quickly** (no more than 5 minutes) what you intend to write, jotting down **four or five supporting quotations.**
- Refer closely to the **key words** in the question.
- Make sure you comment on **what** the author does, the **tecÚiques** he uses and the **effect** of those tecÚiques.
- Support your points with **well-chosen quotations** or other evidence.
- Develop your points by **'zooming in'** on particular **words** or **phrases** and explaining their **effect**.
- Be **persuasive** and **convincing** in what you say.
- Check carefully for **spelling, punctuation** and **grammar.**

PROGRESS LOG [tick the correct box]   Needs more work ☐   Getting there ☐   Under control ☐

Further questions

1 To what extent do you think Dickens is successful in achieving his aim of raising 'the Ghost of an Idea'?

2 To what extent are form and structure important in *A Christmas Carol*?

3 Choose one or two of the minor characters, such as Belle, Fezziwig or Mrs Dilber and discuss their significance to the novella. (You can write about a character not listed here.)

4 How does Dickens present Bob Cratchit and what is his role in the novella?

5 There are several themes in the novella, such as responsibility and kindness. What do you think is the most important theme and why? (You can write about a theme not listed here.)

PROGRESS LOG [tick the correct box]   Needs more work ☐   Getting there ☐   Under control ☐

ANSWERS

NOTE: Answers have been provided for most tasks. Exceptions are 'Practice tasks' and tasks which ask you to write a paragraph or to use your own words or judgement.

PART TWO: PLOT AND ACTION [pp. 8–36]

The Preface & Stave One, pp. 1–3 [pp. 8–9]

1 a) F; b) T; c) T; d) F; e) T; f) T

2 a) The Preface hints at the ghostly aspects of the story to come, but also tells us that it is not meant to be a frightening story. It shows us that Dickens intends to convey a serious message.

b) Dickens emphasises that Marley is dead so that the reader understands that he is a ghost when he appears to Scrooge. Describing Marley's character and the circumstances of his death also allows Dickens to begin to show Scrooge's character.

c) The weather is very cold; it is already dark (at 3 p.m.) and it is foggy.

3

Point/detail	Evidence	Effect or explanation
1: Dickens shows us that Scrooge was not particularly upset by Marley's death, despite their close relationship.	'Scrooge was … his sole friend and sole mourner. And even Scrooge was not so dreadfully cut up'	The repetition of 'sole' emphasises the isolation of Scrooge and Marley; Dickens makes Scrooge's reaction to Marley's death more shocking by placing it in a new sentence.
2: Dickens explains how other people avoid Scrooge.	'No beggars implored him to bestow a trifle'	Scrooge is well known for being mean; everyone knows it is not worth approaching him.
3: Dickens uses detailed description and imagery to present Scrooge's character.	'Hard and sharp as flint, from which no steel had ever struck out generous fire'	Scrooge is shown as having no warmth or softness to his character. Even though flint is hard, it can be used to make fire, but Scrooge seems to have no such side to him.

Stave One, pp. 3–10 [pp. 10–11]

1 Scrooge does not seem to **trust** his clerk, Bob Cratchit, as he does not allow him to have the coal near him. Scrooge's **nephew**, Fred, visits him to wish him '**merry Christmas**' but Scrooge replies with '**Bah!**' and '**Humbug!**' Scrooge thinks that Fred is foolish to celebrate and says 'what reason have you to be merry? You're **poor** enough'. Fred replies that Scrooge should therefore be happy as he is **rich**. Fred thinks of Christmas as a **good** time but cannot convince Scrooge. After he leaves, two **portly** gentlemen visit to try to collect money for the Poor. Scrooge shocks them by suggesting that if the Poor would rather **die** than go to prison or the workhouse, they should do it and **reduce** the **surplus** population.

2 a) We see Bob's happiness and enjoyment of Christmas, while Scrooge, by following his usual routine, emphasises his desire to 'leave it alone' (p. 5).

b) The carol singer gives us another chance to see Scrooge behaving unreasonably towards someone who is simply acting in keeping with the season.

c) Dickens wants this story to portray his views about the unfairness of the Poor Laws and show how the poor are treated. He tries to make readers associate these ideas with Scrooge, whom he is presenting as an unreasonable and negative character.

3

Point/detail	Evidence	Effect or explanation
1: The weather worsens, becoming foggier, darker and colder.	'overflowings sullenly congealed, and turned to misanthropic ice'	This choice of vocabulary reminds the reader of Scrooge, who is both 'sullen' and 'misanthropic', associating him with cold and with being separated from others.
2: Dickens presents a series of festive snapshots, reminding the reader that it is Christmas Eve.	'Poulterers and grocers' trades became … a glorious pageant'	Festive language, such as 'pageant', creates an image of simple shop windows transformed into an amazing display of religious significance.
3: Dickens creates an image of everyone else getting ready to celebrate, in contrast with Scrooge.	'even the little tailor'	By insisting that everyone else is celebrating, Dickens creates a sense of Scrooge being isolated in his attitudes. This creates tension for the reader, preparing us for the action that is to come.

Stave One, pp. 10–20 [pp. 12–13]

1 a) particular; b) lobster; c) stomach; d) forged; e) benevolence

2 a) Dickens insists upon Scrooge's unimaginative nature to make sure the reader believes in the Ghosts, and does not waste time questioning whether they are supposed to be real or not.

b) Dickens refers to him as 'the Ghost' rather than 'Marley' to remind the reader that it is a ghost and not a physical person. Dickens wants the story to be spooky and enjoyable, as well as have a moral message.

c) This Stave's most important purpose is to set up the coming of the Spirits in the following Staves. It is important that readers (and Scrooge) understand that the Spirits have a purpose and that if Scrooge does not learn something from them, he will be condemned like Marley.

3

Point/detail	Evidence	Effect or explanation
1: We see that Scrooge is frightened and uncertain.	'Scrooge fell upon his knees'	Dickens shows how Scrooge's reactions to Marley's revelations grow stronger and stronger as he becomes more disturbed.
2: The construction of Marley's chains is described.	'link by link, and yard by yard'	Dickens's use of repetition emphasises the length of time taken to forge the chains, increasing the reader's sense of dread that this is leading to bad news for Scrooge.

3: The idea of punishment or justice is introduced.	'condemned to do so ... doomed'	Dickens's use of language here is strongly associated with both the law and religion to indicate that Marley's punishment is deserved. The reader is given the impression that whatever is coming to Scrooge is similarly justified.

Stave Two, pp. 21–5 [pp. 14–15]

1 a) T; b) F; c) F; d) T; e) T; f) F

2 a) Dickens is perhaps implying that Scrooge has tried to avoid the Spirits, but is unable to because they have the power to change time if necessary.

b) This tecÚique reminds us that *A Christmas Carol* is like a fireside story, and is suited to being read aloud to an audience. The sense of closeness increases the impact of the story.

c) Dickens is perhaps suggesting here that Scrooge does not wish to face his past or is unable to confront the Ghost's message for him.

3

Point/detail	Evidence	Effect or explanation
1: The Ghost's physical appearance recalls all ages at once.	'like a child: yet not so like a child as like an old man'	This phrasing encourages the reader to see the Ghost as representing an entire lifespan all at once: the whole past of an individual.
2: Dickens refers to distance more than once in describing the Ghost.	'the appearance of having receded from the view'; 'as if ... it were at a distance'	Dickens seems to be presenting the Ghost as embodying the idea of the past by seeming far away and difficult to reach.
3: Dickens emphasises the Ghost's qualities of indistinctness and impermanence.	'the figure itself fluctuated in its distinctness'; 'of which dissolving parts, no outline would be visible'	Through this insistence on the uncertainty of the Ghost's qualities, Dickens reminds us of the nature of memory and the past, which can be difficult to recall exactly, with memories changing over time.

Stave Two, pp. 25–30 [pp. 16–17]

1 The Ghost takes Scrooge into the **countryside** and the atmosphere shifts: the **air** clears and Scrooge's mood changes too. The Ghost asks Scrooge why his voice is **trembling** and there are several hints that he is **crying**. Scrooge and the Ghost visit a schoolroom, passing several happy and excited **children** on the way. Inside the school, just one boy remains, engrossed in **reading**, as characters from the stories appear at the window. The scene shifts to a year later: the same boy, Scrooge, is again **alone** in the school, when his sister, Fan, bursts in to tell him that his **father** has decided that he can return home for Christmas and that he is to become a man.

2 a) Dickens is engaging with the Victorian belief that the countryside was more wholesome and healthy than the city, and to show that Scrooge has not always been the same.

b) We begin to feel sorry for the child who is not treated as well as the others; while others skip home in excitement for Christmas, his only friends are to be found in books.

c) Scrooge will be leaving school and taking up an apprenticeship, to enter the world of work.

3

Point/detail	Evidence	Effect or explanation
1: Dickens presents Fan as small and lively.	'clapping her tiny hands, and bending down to laugh'	Dickens's descriptions of Fan centre on verbs such as 'darting', 'bending' and 'laughing', showing how she is constantly active.
2: Fan is described as a loving sister, keen to have Scrooge back home.	'stood on tiptoe to embrace him'	Although emphasising physical differences between them, Dickens creates an image of Fan as trying to be close to Scrooge.
3: Dickens portrays Scrooge as troubled when the Ghost mentions his nephew.	'Scrooge seemed uneasy in his mind'	Once the Ghost mentions Fred to Scrooge, both Scrooge and the reader are reminded of his rejection of his friendly nephew in the first Stave.

Stave Two, pp. 30–4 [pp. 18–19]

1 a) excited; b) willingly; c) lots of different people; d) skilled and energetic; e) guilty

2 a) Fezziwig's large size and 'oily' voice support his generosity and kindness. He is, to an extent, a larger-than-life character, who shows that being benevolent to others does not require cutting back for oneself.

b) Fezziwig does not simply spend or give money to help others, but he expends effort to enrich others' lives – arguably a more difficult and more worthwhile endeavour.

c) Scrooge's speech prompts us to believe that he is beginning to see the light and that he can be redeemed.

3

Point/detail	Evidence	Effect or explanation
1: We see that Fezziwig has invited many who could be seen as deserving or disadvantaged.	'the boy from over the way, who was suspected of not having board enough from his master'	Dickens models virtuous behaviour through Fezziwig – it is much more effective than preaching to the audience.
2: Dickens uses repetitive structures in his writing in this passage.	'In came ... In came ... In came ...'; 'some shyly, some boldly, some gracefully, some awkwardly, some pushing, some pulling'	These repetitive structures emphasise that this is Fezziwig's habit, as well as that his guests are many and varied. Dickens is showing that the effects of Fezziwig's bounty or kindness are wide ranging.

3: *Dickens seems to want to focus on the relationship between apprentices and their masters or mistresses in this part of the story.*	*'not having board enough from his master … had her ears pulled by her Mistress'*	*Here Dickens raises awareness of the specific issue of how apprentices are treated. He does this indirectly, through Fezziwig's opinion that some employers are negligent, and so we are also encouraged to view such behaviour negatively.*

Stave Two, pp. 34–9 [pp. 20–1]

1 a) F; b) T; c) F; d) T; e) T

2 a) In breaking off the engagement Belle gives us a reason to feel sympathy for Scrooge, but it also allows us to hear another character explaining how he has changed. Belle explains that he hasn't always thought money is the most important thing, and suggests that if they had met 'now', they would not have become engaged.

b) The narrator's appearance allows Dickens to comment straightforwardly on Belle and her family without the complications of Scrooge's emotions and without being too judgemental.

c) Scrooge appears overwhelmed at the end of this scene and acts almost instinctively in pressing down the cap. He doesn't want to see any more.

3

Point/detail	Evidence	Effect or explanation
1: Belle's husband is struck by Scrooge's isolation.	'Quite alone in the world'	Dickens shows that Belle's husband does not think of Scrooge as anything to do with himself or his family: he is merely an object of gossip, having isolated himself by his attitudes.
2: Scrooge wants to get away from the scene; he has had enough of the Ghost's visions.	'"Remove me!" Scrooge exclaimed. "I cannot bear it!"'	Scrooge is pleading now, shown by the exclamation marks. Although earlier visions have affected him, the cumulative effect is overwhelming.
3: Scrooge appears to act without thinking in his panic at this point.	'dimly connecting that with its influence over him'	Dickens emphasises Scrooge's lack of clear thinking here with the adverb 'dimly', which is juxtaposed with the Ghost's light 'burning high and bright'.

Stave Three, pp. 40–7 [pp. 22–3]

1 Scrooge awakens just before the clock strikes **one** and pulls back the curtains around the bed in readiness for the next Spirit. The narrator assures us that he is ready for **anything**, but he is not ready for **nothing**, which is what appears. Eventually, Scrooge gets up to investigate a **light** which is streaming onto the **bed** from the next room, to find a mass of greenery, a piled-up feast and a 'jolly **Giant**'. He is taken around the streets to see people making final preparations for Christmas. Some are taking their dinners to the **baker** to be cooked, as they do not have an oven. The Spirit has a torch, from which he sprinkles incense onto some people and their **dinners**.

2 a) Scrooge is unafraid as he has not yet really changed. Although he did react to the Ghost of Christmas Past, it was just 'in the moment': he has not yet undergone meaningful, lasting change.

b) Dickens uses a great deal of white and black in this section to contrast the rich and poor houses with their beautiful untouched snow or filthy soot. He also shows lots of brightly coloured food and greenery put out for the season.

c) The Spirit's incense is most strongly applied to the dinners of the poorest because they need and deserve it the most. This is part of Dickens's theme of poverty and how it should not be overlooked.

3

Point/detail	Evidence	Effect or explanation
1: Scrooge argues against closing eating establishments on Sundays because the poor may not be able to eat well on other days.	'often the only day on which they can be said to dine at all'	This encourages the reader to think about why poorer families would find it difficult to 'dine' on the other days of the week.
2: The Spirit is offended that Scrooge blames him for this.	'"I!" cried the Spirit.'	Dickens is encouraging readers to think about the effect of closing businesses on Sundays, and about how this links to the idea of spirituality.
3: Dickens makes the Spirit list a number of sins which are committed by humans and blamed on the Spirits.	'and who do their deeds of passion, pride … in our name, who are as strange to us and all our kith and kin, as if they had never lived'	Dickens wants the reader to realise that, simply because a person claims to do something in the name of a god or spirit, that does not make it true, or morally correct. He wants his readers to think for themselves about what is right.

Stave Three, pp. 47–53 [pp. 24–5]

1 a) brave; b) tearing; c) thoughtful; d) eked out; e) cannon-ball; f) Founder

2 a) The Cratchits' family life seems to be loving and happy: the children are all helping their mother prepare for dinner and are happy to see their father return. Martha cannot bear to disappoint her father for long by pretending not to be there.

b) Mrs Cratchit, like all the Cratchits, is seen to be grateful despite having very little, so her angry outburst against Scrooge has all the more weight.

c) The Spirit reminds Scrooge – and the reader – about his callous words about the 'surplus population' in order to encourage him to change and to help us to see that change in him. Connecting these words to a specific family (whom he knows) also make it more difficult for Scrooge to hold this belief.

3

Point/detail	Evidence	Effect or explanation
1: The Cratchits are amused by the idea of Peter working in business.	'The two young Cratchits laughed tremendously at the idea of Peter's being a man of business'	Dickens shows us that even though the family needs the money, it is not the most important thing to them and they are a happy family even without it, unlike Scrooge.

2: The world of work and business is presented as separate and unfamiliar to the Cratchits.	'bewildering income'; 'Martha … then told them what kind of work she had to do'	In the Cratchits' life, work is presented as something done as a means to an end. Dickens is perhaps showing how the poor must toil at hard, uninspiring work in order to survive.
3: Dickens contrasts their poor appearance with their cheerfulness and obvious love for one another.	'they were not well dressed … But they were happy, grateful, pleased with one another'	By presenting the Cratchit family in this way, Dickens contrasts their low social position with their happiness.

Stave Three, pp. 54–64 [pp. 26–7]

1 a) F; b) T; c) F; d) T; e) F; f) T

2 a) Dickens shows a range of different people celebrating in order to underline the idea that Scrooge is isolated in his approach to Christmas, and to show that the poor can celebrate family togetherness.

b) Fred's views about Scrooge seem to be intended to encourage readers to have some empathy for Scrooge: he is unreasonable, but he is also creating a miserable existence for himself, and denying himself joy.

c) Dickens reminds both Scrooge and the reader that the purpose of the Spirits' visits is redemption. Scrooge has said, thought and done some terrible things and he must be made to see that in order to change his ways and live a better life.

3

Point/detail	Evidence	Effect or explanation
1: Dickens presents Ignorance and Want as appalling and frightening creatures, emphasising how they are different from what children should be.	'Where angels might have sat enthroned, devils lurked'	Dickens presents these characters as corrupted or twisted by what has happened to them. They could have been happy, healthy children, but Man has made them terrifying creatures.
2: Scrooge is shocked at their appearance and does not know what to say.	'Scrooge could say no more.'	Scrooge is rarely lost for words and appears hard-hearted at the start of the novella especially, so his reaction here shows how very shocking their appearance is.
3: Dickens created these characters to argue that humanity has created the problem of poverty (want) through a lack of education (ignorance).	'Beware them both … but most of all beware this boy'	Dickens is showing the reader that ignorance, or lack of education, is the cause of many other problems in his society. He was a supporter of free education for the poor, believing that this would help to improve their situation.

Stave Four, pp. 65–75 [pp. 28–9]

1 a) 2; b) 6; c) 4; d) 3; e) 1; f) 5

2 a) This Spirit is silent and merely points to direct Scrooge's attention. It therefore appears more serious or gloomy than the previous ones.

b) Scrooge seems to feel that he may be the dead man, since he keeps looking for himself but cannot see himself anywhere. The reader may wonder at the mention of bed-curtains and the repeated description of the man as alone and focused only on money and business.

c) The description of the young couple emphasises the dead man's isolation, since there is no one who misses him or feels any emotion on his death except this family who feel only relief at having a little longer to pay a debt. This scenario strongly underlines both the general human consequences of money-lending and Scrooge's specific lack of human connections.

3

Point/detail	Evidence	Effect or explanation
1: The thieves suggest that the dead man should have formed more relationships in life, in order to have people to leave things to.	'If he wanted to keep 'em after he was dead … why wasn't he natural in his lifetime?'	Even the thieves see the dead man's behaviour as unnatural, which they believe makes him fair game for their thievery.
2: Dickens uses vocabulary describing value and cost in presenting what the thieves' haul is worth.	'appraised'; 'the sums he was disposed to give for each'	This emphasises that the man's life ultimately comes down only to monetary value, since he has failed to make anything else of it.
3: Dickens suggests that the dead man's behaviour has ultimately benefited only the thieves, as no one cares enough to notice their theft.	'He frightened every one away from him when he was alive, to profit us when he was dead!'	This shows that, whatever the man's intentions, his actions have had only negative results, and produced no positive outcomes.

Stave Four, pp. 76–80 [pp. 30–1]

1 a) colour; b) not carrying Tiny Tim; c) cheerful; d) buried; e) kindness; f) neglected

2 a) Dickens shows us a very quiet Cratchit household, so we can tell that something is wrong. He hints that Mrs Cratchit has been crying and wishes to hide it from her husband and the narrator shows understanding of the situation.

b) Dickens reminds us of Fred to show that wealthy people can be good, that kindness is not only about spending money, and that it can mean a great deal to people.

c) Scrooge thinks that he has changed already and therefore his future should have changed already too.

3

Point/detail	Evidence	Effect or explanation
1: Tiny Tim's influence on the lives of others is long-lasting and has a profound effect.	'we shall none of us forget poor Tiny Tim'	Tiny Tim is discussed in affectionate terms, with the family using absolute and definitive language such as 'shall' and 'none of us'. Dickens clearly intends Tiny Tim to live on in readers' memories.

2: Bob Cratchit remembers Tiny Tim's good qualities.	'how patient and how mild he was'	Dickens uses Bob to make a point about being good, emphasised by the repeated 'how' here and showing that Tiny Tim seems to have an instructive role for his family.
3: Tiny Tim's role is to remind everyone to be grateful and happy, no matter what their situation is.	'we shall not quarrel easily among ourselves, and forget poor Tiny Tim in doing it'	Dickens is using Tiny Tim's character in a way that would be familiar for the Victorian audience, who were accustomed to seeing disabled characters used as moral lessons.

Stave Five, pp. 81–5 [pp. 32–3]

1 a) T; b) F; c) T; d) F; e) T; f) T

2 a) Scrooge repeats 'I will live in the Past, the Present, and the Future!' to show that he has learned the lessons of all three Ghosts, and that he will not forget. This repetition also supports the episodic nature of the narrative.

b) Scrooge's struggle to get dressed adds comedy and shows his excitement but also delays the final resolution of the story.

c) Scrooge's desire to send the Cratchits a turkey without his name shows that he just wants them to enjoy a turkey, not that he wants credit for providing it. This proves the purity of his intention.

3

Point/detail	Evidence	Effect or explanation
1: Scrooge acts strangely, showing confusion and uncertainty.	'laughing and crying in the same breath'	This is completely unlike his behaviour at the start of the novella, when he is very certain in his views.
2: Scrooge uses language which shows he is ready for a new beginning.	'I'm quite a baby'	This metaphor invokes the idea of being born again, familiar to Christian believers in the Victorian period.
3: Dickens uses similar language techniques in Scrooge's speech and in his narration.	'"Never mind. I don't care." ... Clash, clang, hammer, ding, dong'	Dickens's use of short sentences in both Scrooge's speech and the narration implies that Scrooge is now more in tune with his surroundings.

Stave Five, pp. 85–8 [pp. 34–5]

1 'Scrooge was better than his word. He did it all, and **infinitely** more; and to Tiny Tim, who did NOT die, he was a second **father**. He became as good a friend, as good a **master**, and as good a man, as the **good** old city knew, or any other **good** old city, town or borough, in the **good** old world. Some people laughed to see the alteration in him, but he let them laugh, and little heeded them; for he was **wise** enough to know that nothing ever happened on this globe, for good, at which some people did not have their fill of **laughter** in the outset.'

2 a) Fred welcomes Scrooge because this shows Fred's goodness and that he believes in the importance of the family and is always ready to accept Scrooge into his home.

b) Bob wants to call for 'help and a strait-waistcoat' because his first thought is that Scrooge has become mentally unstable.

c) Dickens ends with the narrator's voice because this fits with the genre of a story told aloud and enables Dickens to tie up loose ends and speed over many years to reach the ending.

3

Point/detail	Evidence	Effect or explanation
1: The narrator first comments on Scrooge's niece.	'Dear heart alive, how his niece by marriage started!'	The narrator's use of exclamatory language echoes Fred's wife's shocked reaction, and adds impact. At the same time, the phrase 'Dear heart alive' is very gentle and offers connotations of warmth and even love.
2: Sometimes the narrator's language echoes Scrooge's thought patterns.	'If he could only be there first'	Dickens uses the narrator to enable the audience to see what Scrooge is thinking. This happens more towards the end of the novella, when Scrooge is more sympathetic, than at the start.
3: The narrator is the storyteller but may also represent the reader: an ordinary person responding to this extraordinary tale.	'Let him in! It is a mercy he didn't shake his arm off.'	The narrator often reacts as the audience might. His surprise here, shown by the exclamatory sentence 'Let him in!', shows the audience that surprise is the proper response.

PART THREE: CHARACTERS [pp. 37–42]

Who's who? [p. 37]

a) Ebenezer Scrooge; b) Fred; c) Marley's Ghost; d) Ghost of Christmas Yet to Come; e) Ignorance and Want; f) Ghost of Christmas Past; g) Tiny Tim; h) Fan; i) Belle; j) Bob Cratchit; k) Ghost of Christmas Present; l) Mr Fezziwig

Marley's Ghost [p. 38]

1

Quality	In life or as Ghost?	Moment(s) in novella	Quotation
An excellent businessman	Life	Scrooge does not understand why Marley is critical of himself in life when he was a success.	'But you were always a good man of business, Jacob!'
Keen to help Scrooge	Ghost	Marley explains that he has set up Scrooge's visit from the three Ghosts in order to help him.	'I am here to-night to warn you, that you have yet a chance and hope of escaping my fate.'
Greedy	Life	The visit of the charity collectors	Scrooge and Marley 'had been two kindred spirits'

Remorseful	Ghost	Marley tells Scrooge that he cannot help people now and wishes he had done so when he was alive.	'Why did I walk through crowds of fellow-beings with my eyes turned down...?'

Ebenezer Scrooge [p. 39]

2 • from which no steel had ever struck out generous fire – mean = he never gave away anything

• The cold within him froze his old features – callous = he is so cold in spirit that he is cold in body too

Fred [p. 40]

1, 2 optimistic (p. 59), playful (p. 4), jolly (p. 56), kind (p. 77), generous (p. 86), loving (p. 86), respectful (p. 6), affectionate (p. 4), cheerful (p. 5), forgiving (p. 58)

Bob [p. 40]

1 • praised the industry and speed of Mrs Cratchit and the girls – attentive = despite his upsetting experience, he is careful to praise his wife and daughters

• It would have done you good to see how green a place it is – loving = aware of his wife's needs

The Ghosts of Christmas [p. 41]

1

	Physical attributes	Effect on and interaction with Scrooge	Attitude to and interaction with others
The Ghost of Christmas Past	Brightly-lit, ever-changing, represents all the past phases of Scrooge	Questions Scrooge about why Fezziwig's generosity matters	Shows Scrooge visions that are personal and specific to him
The Ghost of Christmas Present	Large and jolly, wearing a green fur-trimmed mantle (with Want and Ignorance hiding underneath it)	Repeats Scrooge's cruel words back to him	Sprinkles a special incense on all meals, especially 'poor' ones; shows Scrooge many different people
The Ghost of Christmas Yet to Come	Faceless and hooded	Does not speak, only points; delays revealing that the dead man is Scrooge	Presents Scrooge with bleak and unpleasant visions

2 a) Dickens sets up the religious implications of Marley's Ghost, with the suggestion that his haunting is a judgement or punishment for the life he lived. The lessons taught by the Ghosts are moral ones, and Marley states that Scrooge can change the kind of afterlife that he will have by acting now. Scrooge also refers to the Sabbath as belonging to the Ghosts (i.e. God or the Church), but the Ghost of Christmas Present definitively rejects this idea.

b) Dickens creates symbolism in many ways, e.g. through invoking the familiar imagery of Death in the future Ghost. He also makes the Ghost of the Past indistinct and the Ghost of the Present short-lived, as the present is only ever a fleeting moment, quickly becoming past. The light emitting from the Ghost of the Past seems to suggest that memory may offer clarity or understanding, while the Ghost of the Present's torch offers incense which may symbolise generosity or love.

PART FOUR: THEMES, CONTEXTS AND SETTINGS [pp. 43–50]

Themes [pp. 43–5]

1 a) responsibility; b) education; c) poverty; d) the supernatural; e) isolation

2 As well as using his novella to show how it is morally **wrong** to assume the poor are inadequate or lazy, Dickens also uses his characters to show that **money/wealth** does not automatically bring happiness. The characters in *A Christmas Carol* who are happy are clearly shown to be so by their **nature**, not because of material wealth. Both Fred and Bob love their families and are happy, but materially and in terms of social **class** they are very different. Dickens therefore does not wish his readers to conclude that it is Fred's **wealth** which enables him to be happy, as otherwise Bob could not also show a **similar** positive outlook.

3 a) This comment shows how Mr Fezziwig represents generosity in Scrooge's past, because he is kind to all around him, including those he is not directly responsible for. Dickens uses the verb 'suspected' to show that Mr Fezziwig does not need to be certain of the boy's need for help before he offers it.

b) Dickens uses the Ghost of Christmas Present's torch to show Scrooge (and the audience) that generosity needs to be offered according to need. This is clearly indicated through the repetition of 'most', which also has the effect of making the need seem urgent, and yet Scrooge is unable to recognise this and needs the Ghost to explain it to him.

c) Despite Tim's own poor condition in the novella, he is concerned about others and his effect upon them above all else. He represents the very spirit of generosity, emphasised further by the fact that Dickens makes this a reported event, rather than one we see directly. Since Bob tells us about Tim's words, this adds an impression of humility to the one of generosity, as we view Tim's words through the lens of Bob's wonder at Tim's generosity of spirit.

4 a) Scrooge seems happy to be alone at the start of the story. However, this is not the case when the Ghost of Christmas Past takes him back to his childhood. Scrooge is quite upset as he sees himself alone reading in the schoolroom.

b) Dickens suggests that the effects of isolation multiply, as the future Scrooge is clearly even more isolated than the Scrooge who moves through the story.

c) Scrooge is transformed in terms of the theme of isolation, since at the start of the story he shuns the company of others, but seeks it out at the end. For example, he visits Fred and his family and enjoys speaking to strangers in the street.

ANSWERS

5

Point/detail	Evidence	Effect or explanation
1: *Marley explains that Spirits must make up for what they failed to do in life.*	*'condemned to do so after death'*	*This sets up the idea that Scrooge would have something to make up for and therefore needs redemption.*
2: *Marley shows Scrooge his chains and makes Scrooge believe that his would be even longer and heavier.*	*'It was full as heavy and as long as this, seven Christmas Eves ago. You have laboured on it, since.'*	*Dickens is emphasising that Scrooge would have to endure the same punishment as Marley but even more so.*
3: *Marley shows Scrooge a host of Spirits filling the night air.*	*'The air filled with phantoms, wandering hither and thither'*	*This supports Marley's claims and shows to Scrooge (and the audience) that Marley's predicament is not an isolated one, and affects all Mankind.*

Contexts [pp. 46–7]

1 a) T; b) F; c) T; d) F; e) T

2 a) the countryside and London; b) the Poor Laws;
c) blacking factory; d) a debtors' prison

3 a) Dickens shows us that the Cratchits are poor through their clothing, their food and their home. For example, Mrs Cratchit is described as 'brave in ribbons', because she has tried to get dressed up for Christmas but does not have any smart clothes.

b) Dickens makes it clear that, in life, Marley's views were the same as Scrooge's, but he also shows that Marley desperately regrets this position, as do the other Spirits that Scrooge sees at the end of Stave One. Dickens is also careful not to show any other living characters who seem to share Scrooge's views, leaving the reader with an impression of Scrooge's views as unusual.

Settings [pp. 48–9]

1 a) Fred's Christmas party; b) Marley's Ghost visits Scrooge;
c) Scrooge discovers he is the man who died; d) Scrooge mistreats Bob Cratchit in various ways; e) People sell items taken from the dead man; f) The Cratchits celebrate Christmas together

2 a) Dickens's descriptions of happy homes (Belle's family, the Cratchit family, Fred's family) all display a generous and giving attitude towards others, but it is worth noting that they are not all wealthy homes, as Dickens would not have wanted to give the impression that only the wealthy can be happy.

b) Dickens uses the weather as a setting, particularly at the start and finish of the novella. In the opening Stave, there is much description of the 'cold, bleak, biting weather', which is also foggy and makes it difficult to see, while the novella ends on a clear, bright winter's day, symbolically showing Scrooge's path from darkness to light.

PART FIVE: FORM, STRUCTURE AND LANGUAGE [pp. 51–7]

Form [p. 51]

1 *A Christmas Carol* is written to evoke the fireside tales format, and specifically that of a **ghost** story. Dickens uses **Staves** instead of chapters, perhaps to show that he is **experimenting** or playing with form, rather than writing a serious story. He wanted this story to be heard by many people, because its core **message** was very important to him. In keeping with the ghost story form, Dickens uses an **intrusive** narrator who often comments on the action and reminds us that we are listening to (or reading) a story. This form also allows him to write in a **dramatic** and sometimes **exaggerated** way, as well as making some things possible that would otherwise be **unrealistic**. Finally, the moral message is delivered in a **direct** way, with a threat of eternal punishment, and yet the message is given with warmth and **humour**.

2 a) The insight Scrooge gains – into many other people's homes and his own past, as well as the future – would be impossible to achieve as convincingly in a more realistic narrative without the existence of the Ghosts.

b) A novella is a complete story which is longer than a short story but shorter than a novel. In this case, Dickens keeps the plot tightly focused on Scrooge – there is, for example, no subplot and there is only one reversal.

Structure [pp. 52–3]

1 a) precipitating incident; b) rising action; c) climax; d) epiphany;
e) standard

2

Stave One	Stave Five
Scrooge refuses to give money to the portly gentlemen.	Scrooge gives the portly gentlemen a large sum of money, including 'a great many back-payments'.
Scrooge rejects Fred's offer to dine with him for Christmas.	Scrooge goes to Fred's house for Christmas dinner.
Scrooge complains about Bob wanting the whole day off with pay for Christmas.	Scrooge raises Bob's salary.

3

Point/detail	Evidence	Effect or explanation
1: *The narrator emphasises Marley's present status as dead.*	*'Marley was dead: to begin with.'*	*The additional phrase 'to begin with' explains that he is dead before the story starts, while implying that he does not remain dead.*
2: *The narrator discusses the idea of being dead at length.*	*'I might have been inclined, myself, to regard a coffin-nail as the deadest piece of ironmongery in the trade.'*	*The gently humorous tone, engaging in wordplay with the simile 'dead as a doornail' by substituting the noun 'coffin' for 'door' shows the reader that this will not be an entirely serious story in tone, while emphatically remaining on the topic of death.*
3: *The reader is directed to focus on Marley being dead, but the role of ghosts and haunting is foreshadowed.*	*'Hamlet's Father … taking a stroll'*	*Dickens's reference to Hamlet encourages the reader to infer that ghosts will play a part in the tale.*

Language [pp. 54–6]

1 a) simile; b) listing; c) adjective; d) personification; e) adverb

2 a) Dickens uses a considerable amount of weather imagery in setting up the story partially as a convention of ghost stories and partially to introduce the idea of Scrooge's emotional coldness.

b) Scrooge's bed is a focus at the beginning of the central Staves, with Scrooge awakening and awaiting the Ghosts there. The bed, usually a person's most private refuge, is intruded upon by these spiritual visitors and then, in the vision of the future, it is violated by Mrs Dilber's disrespectful theft, symbolising Scrooge's personal battle.

3

Intrusive narration	Quotation	Analysis or explanation
1: *Dickens uses the intrusive narrator to conform to the fireside ghost story genre.*	*'Once upon a time – of all the good days in the year, on Christmas Eve – old Scrooge sat busy in his counting-house.'*	*The traditional and timeless storytelling structure of 'once upon a time' is combined with a specific time 'Christmas Eve', to provide the story with a more particular setting.*
2: *Dickens uses the intrusive narrator to make judgemental comments about Scrooge.*	*'Oh! But he was a tight-fisted hand at the grindstone, Scrooge!'*	*Using the intrusive narrator allows Dickens to criticise Scrooge in a spoken tone, e.g. using the exclamatory 'oh!' and beginning sentences with connectives such as 'but'.*
3: *Dickens uses the intrusive narrator to help the audience understand more than Scrooge.*	*'The colour? Ah, poor Tiny Tim!'*	*Here, the narrator implicitly makes the connection between Mrs Cratchit's 'weak eyes' and what has happened to Tiny Tim, leading the audience to do the same.*

4 • I – (repeated) pronoun = emphasis on own responsibility for predicament
   • the chain I forged in life – imagery = metaphor of chain constructed of guilt made physical

5

Point/detail	Evidence	Effect or explanation
1: *Short sentences*	*'Yes! And the bedpost was his own.'*	*These reveal his straightforward thought processes as he celebrates being returned safely.*
2: *Repetition and near-repetition*	*'They are not torn down ... they are not torn down, rings and all. They are here: I am here'*	*Dickens uses repetition here to show that Scrooge is flustered and trying to reassure himself that the negative future has not happened and can be avoided.*
3: *Lists*	*'turning them inside out, putting them on upside down, tearing them, mislaying them'*	*In contrast with the earlier Scrooge who was precise and carefully followed routine, Dickens now shows Scrooge performing many contradictory actions one after another in this list of verbs. This demonstrates how completely different Scrooge now is.*

PART SIX: PROGRESS BOOSTER [pp. 58–71]

Expressing and explaining ideas [pp. 58–9]

2 Student A: Mid

The student supports their argument with evidence, shows an understanding of the text and some writer's techniques. The answer lacks depth or detail, however.

Student B: High

This student labels language precisely and comments on the specific effect on the reader of the narrator's intrusion.

3 The phrase 'teeth were chattering' suggests both cold and fear, contributing to the sense of foreboding.

4, 5, 6 Dickens **portrays** Scrooge's absolute inability to have empathy for the poor through the climax to his conversation with the 'portly gentlemen'. When Scrooge **states** that they should 'decrease the surplus population' by dying, this not only **demonstrates** his lack of understanding, but it also **indicates** that he sees them as less than human, since he **reveals** no human feeling for them at all.

Making inferences and interpretations [p. 60]

1 Towards the end of Stave Four, Scrooge <u>wants to see 'what I shall be, in days to come'</u>. This reveals Scrooge's lack of understanding of the process he is undergoing: he feels that he has already changed and, therefore, that the vision of himself in the future will reflect this change. This suggests that he has not understood that the process which Marley set in motion for his redemption has not yet been completed, and he has some way to go before his future self can be saved.

2 b) ... Scrooge is beginning to understand his own responsibility and the effect his actions have on others.

Writing about context [p. 61]

1 b) It makes the link between Scrooge's home at this time and his character.

2 a) *'And the Union workhouses?' demanded Scrooge. 'Are they still in operation?'* This shows his firm belief in government policy and Malthusian economic theory.

Structure and linking of paragraphs [pp. 62–3]

1 <u>Dickens presents the Ghosts as guides who help Scrooge learn from the scenes he is shown.</u> They sometimes highlight his previous bad behaviour in order to do this, for example, repeating Scrooge's words back to him and calling him an 'Insect'. This teaches Scrooge how insignificant he is and demonstrates to him that he does not have the right to judge or criticise others.

3 <u>Dickens presents Scrooge as an older man who seems very set in his ways.</u> At the start of the novella, his ideas about Christmas and other people appear very fixed, for example when he refuses to help 'Idle people', suggesting that he has no sympathy for the poor whatsoever. <u>By the end of the novella, he is transformed.</u> The insights the Ghosts give him into other people's lives make it impossible for him to continue to dehumanise them, which changes his outlook completely.

Writing skills [pp. 64–5]

3 At the beginning of Stave Two, Dickens builds the tension rapidly as Scrooge cannot believe the time from his 'preposterous little clock'. The uncertainty created about the time makes the audience unsure about what is happening and how the ghosts are controlling Scrooge's world. This technique makes the audience sympathise with Scrooge as we feel the same as him.

ANSWERS

4 *Dickens's use of an intrusive narrator in the novella often has the function of reminding the audience that they are reading—or listening to—a story. It is there from the start, e.g. 'Scrooge and he were partners for I don't know how many years'. He may have done this to help emphasise his moral message, about caring for others.*

5 Student B

6 *The Ghost of Christmas Present <u>tries</u> to teach Scrooge by calling him an 'Insect on the leaf' and comparing him to 'his hungry brothers in the dust'. With this metaphor of Scrooge 'on the leaf', Dickens <u>implies</u> that he <u>is</u> lucky to have enough to live on, while the word 'brothers' implicitly <u>connects</u> Scrooge and the poor.*

Tackling exam tasks [p. 66]

1 Question: How does <u>Dickens</u> tackle <u>ideas</u> about <u>social class and poverty</u> in the novella?

Write about:

- <u>Ideas</u> about <u>social class and poverty</u>
- <u>How Dickens presents</u> those ideas

Sample answers [pp. 68–71]

1 Student A: 1 – mid level; Student B: 2 – lower level

3 Student A: 2 – mid level; Student B: 1 – high level